I0763902

# THE HOLLER

A Novel

Bo Hunter

First edition

ISBN: 979-8-9954285-0-3

Published by Kudzu Kid Press
Perry, Georgia

# Table of Contents

# GONE WITH THE FRIED GREEN CRAWDADS

"Please don't be a serial killer," I muttered aloud. Then again, that might finally give me peace of mind or be a better pain reliever than tequila. I looked upward and addressed the sky. "Your call." I'd been muttering to myself—and the big guy, or big whatever, upstairs—more often in recent months as the old home place grew oppressively quieter since my wife and then my beloved daughter walked out on me and the perfect life I mistakenly thought I'd built for them out of my childhood roots, a life they found perfectly abhorrent.

Perhaps renting out my guest house for the summer was a dumb idea, I thought. Oh, who was I kidding? *Of course*, it was dumb. That was my well-established pattern after decades of being considered a genius—with numbers anyway. People, not so much. I was relieved to see a red Prius crawling up my winding dirt driveway. It's a scientific fact that zero percent of serial killers drive Priuses. Still, I approached cautiously. After all, he could be worse than a serial killer. He could be, *gulp*, annoying.

Who the hell drives all the way from Boston University to spend half the summer in itty-bitty Andersonville, Georgia, for a "sociology project" about the South—and why would he offer to pay me extra to interview me throughout his stay? I turned down the extra money because I barely understand the South myself with all its dichotomies and quirks.

I'm not sure how his GPS found my aging farmhouse hidden away from the two-lane blacktop of Highway 228, five miles outside the official city limits of Andersonville. I lived in the same county as Andersonville, Sumter, although I could walk to the Macon County line if ever so inclined. Lately, I hadn't even walked so far as Boggy Branch, which I could see from my back deck as it slithered its way toward Timber Creek. Hell, it had taken my last grain of motivation to roll out of bed on this Sunday, my day of rest.

The little car was eerily clean, like a rolling operating room table. That did strike me as a bit serial killer-y. I was damn sure the car's tires never touched dirt before that day. I suspected the same about the driver who would be my first paying guest in the studio apartment outside my garage. I didn't suspect he'd also be my last.

Folks around here call this area Possum Holler. Georgia has at least twenty other Possum Hollers, making it dang near as popular as Booger Bottom or Garden Valley for a Southern boondocky moniker. We're all into hollers, bottoms, valleys, and other low places around here because we have so few uppity folks.

The U.S. Postal Service deemed my house to be *in* Andersonville, though I doubt the Census Bureau counted me as part of the city's official population—237, the last I'd heard. That's about 236 more neighbors than I wanted. Of course, I doubt any community wanted to count me officially or unofficially, be it Possum Holler, Andersonville, or New York City, though I'd been a resident of each.

The kid couldn't have looked more "you ain't from around here" if he'd been beamed down by Captain Kirk than he did when he stepped out of that go-kart of a vehicle and brushed back his shoulder-length dark brown hair while checking his reflection in the driver's side window. He was painfully skinny. I could send him back home a fat boy if he truly was committed to staying the full six weeks for which he'd already paid. All he had to do was ask me which places my doctor wanted to ban me from.

He looked harmless enough, but so do most serial killers. With khaki pants and a button-down white shirt, he was dressed more appropriately for a job interview or casual Friday at the office instead of a Sunday afternoon in Possum Holler. It was a typically hot end of May afternoon, 94 degrees with whatever kind of humidity is a touch above a hundred percent—"chewy" air, as I call it. It would get much chewier in the coming weeks. The towering pines that shielded the farmhouse from the road sweated out sap while roasted cones committed conifer suicide every few minutes, plunging to their deaths on straw-covered ground that could've used a good raking if anyone gave a crap. I saw those straw-covered areas merely as less to mow. Thunderheads swelled in the western sky as they amassed for the regularly scheduled afternoon storm. I was in my ragged tank-top, shorts and flip-flops—practically formal wear for me on days when I wasn't teaching history at Muckalee Christian Academy, about twelve miles south in Americus. I was long removed from my tie-wearing days on Wall Street, when I once tolerated what my late father described as "Sunday/go-to-meeting clothes." I wondered what my guest was thinking: probably "I hope this guy isn't a serial killer."

His effeminate walk was out of place in Possum Holler, where toddler boys walk like John Wayne. Yet, nothing about his look offered a clue about how his mere arrival in Possum Holler would trigger a chaotic series of events.

This is a story I witnessed much of with my own eyes, while some of the gaps would be filled in by others, including young Mr. Boston himself. There's plenty I don't know about that stretch, and I'm not sure I want to. I don't believe ignorance is bliss, but *too much* knowledge can be brutal, even deadly. Someone may someday fill in the gaps, but it damn sure won't be me. I'm doing my level best to drown those summer memories with the help of my buddies Monte and Jose. I've got plenty to think about and even more to *drink* about. That summer spread the shit brown icing on the vanilla crap cake I'd half-baked with a recipe book of good intentions over the past decade.

"Hi, I'm Jack, Jack Settles," the kid said as he extended his lean right arm for a handshake. "You must be Mr. Peachy."

"I must be, indeed. Ain't got a choice."

No, Peachy is not a nickname given to me by fellow New Yorkers years earlier nor by Ivy League classmates at Brown who knew I hailed from The Peach State. It's my actual last name—two generations following a grandfather who left his Amish roots in the 1940s. I think he invented "spiritual but not religious," but his Amish family was unimpressed with his originality. I bet my great-grandparents would be even less enamored with *my* stance on religion—somewhat spiritual but more "spare me the bullshit." Yet, somewhere deep inside me is a little Amish. I call him Obadiah.

"Ben," I said simply as I gave him a gentle handshake I hadn't used since my up-North days. Most fellas around Possum Holler shake with the intent of causing anything from mild pain to metacarpal fracturing, depending on whether the *shakee* is friend or foe. Most of the guys around here have illegible handwriting by age fifty. Mine is pure scribble. But I thought it'd be rude to injure the kid on day one. "C'mon. I'll show you the place."

"Actually, my real name's John, but folks call me Jack," he said, "kinda like JFK."

"Folks in Boston think John is short for Jack?" I asked. "I guess math hasn't made it up there yet." He seemed taken aback. Maybe he'd never thought about it. Whatever the case, he clearly wasn't used to a dry, albeit rusty, wit like mine that I doled out with the degree of levity you might use when telling your child their dog up and died—a Southern colloquialism that makes about as much sense as calling someone Jack instead of John.

I wasn't out to harass the kid nor portray some stereotypical Southern character from a B horror movie, but I knew Jack was different by Possum Holler standards. Hell, so was I, albeit in other ways. Down South, it takes mental toughness to be an exception in a world of countrified conformity and group-think. He needed a tough skin if he was going to survive a few hot weeks in Possum Holler. I had no intention of mentoring him, mind you, for I already walked a thin line between loving and hating the place and could fall on either side of that line on any given day. I just didn't want him to be blindsided by the assholes. I'm merely a smart ass, not an asshole, although I do speak the language. I figured he had me stereotyped as some *Green Acres* hick, so I might as well have some fun with it.

As we neared the guest house at the end of the driveway catty-cornered from the garage, I suppressed a grin as I noted in the stereotypical Southern drawl that had almost evaporated during my years in New York, "You know, I think you might be the first Yankee we've had in Andersonville since they shut down the prison."

"Since April 1865?" he asked, looking at me like a kindergartner who'd just been told there was a big, bad wolf in the nearby woods. Maybe he was pondering an escape route.

"Ah, history buff? By the way, don't believe everything you've read about Andersonville—especially about any prisoners escaping. Ain't lost one yet." Jack stopped in his tracks four feet from the door and appeared to be weighing whether he could outrun me to his car...as if I'd *run* anywhere. "I'm joking, kid. Is 160 years too soon?"

Jack let out an audible "whew" and followed me through the door. "Wow, this looks comfortable," he said. It definitely was, just not comfy enough to keep my daughter from running off to New York to live with her mom and new Daddy Warbucks stepdad. She considered herself the first prisoner to escape suburban Andersonville—although she was merely the *second* after her mom. I'd made the space into an art studio for my then-wife, Elizabeth. After she bolted, I then spent two years converting it into a damn nice pad for Riley Savannah—complete with a mini-kitchen, full bath, and Murphy bed. There were a couple of armchairs, an old wooden desk, and a small television atop an empty chest of drawers. It's unlikely any teenager in the area had sweeter digs all to themselves, and I doubt any teenager in the area could have been less impressed with their arrangements than was Riley. It's possible she was even less won over than Elizabeth had been with the artist's paradise I'd created with equally good intentions.

"There's a washer and dryer in my garage," I told him. "I doubt we'll have much trouble sharing it this summer. I'm a teacher, and when school's out, my entire wardrobe can fit in a carry-on. The kids are out, and I've just got an admin week left. Oh, the garage code is 1-1-1-1. Be sure to write that down."

"I think I can remember," he responded, dead serious again.

"Damn, you're like some kind of super-genius or something! You've got that little air-conditioner that'll freeze you out of here in just a few minutes, and there's that standing fan you may want when you're sleeping. The wi-fi's pretty good out here—the router's in the garage midway between here and my office."

"Yes, sir. And the password?"

"Grab that paper and pen," I told him as I pointed to the desk. He placed it on the small kitchen counter and prepared to write. "OK, it's capital K-i-l-l-a-y-a-n-k-e-e-1-8-6-1." He paused. "Wait, no, I changed it after the war. Make that capital *B-u-l-l-d-o-g-1-!*. That's probably half the passwords around here, so don't share it with the Russians. By the way, if you need to chill out and relax—which I strongly suggest—there's a beer or twelve in the fridge."

"Thanks," he said. "I don't really drink, but I do vape a little weed every now and then if that's OK."

"Not inside the apartment, Cheech," I insisted. "I hate that damn smell. Can't go anywhere without smelling that crap these days. Why don't you do gummies like normal folks? They're legal in Georgia. They're also more powerful. It's that dirty little secret that the politicians don't know."

"Actually, this doesn't have much of a smell," he insisted. "Kinda skunky-lite."

"Don't care. By the way, if you smell any chemicals from the back of the building, that's just the meth lab. Help yourself."

"Joking?"

"A glimmer of hope. Glad that pot hasn't killed every brain cell. Give it time, though. You're also welcome to use the pool anytime unless I'm swimming. I don't wear a swimsuit, and, well, that'd just be awkward. Impressive, but awkward."

"Joking again. I get it."

"No. A swimsuit would just be one more thing I'd have to wash. I'm gonna take my Sunday nap now, but don't hesitate to ask if you need anything. Actually, *do* hesitate at least an hour."

"Yes, sir."

"By the way, this sociology project of yours—why choose the middle of nowhere Georgia?" I asked. "Haven't people been nowhere before?"

"Everywhere's somewhere," he responded. "I want to experience the *real* South—you know, beyond the stereotypes or Hollywood view or the big cities like Atlanta, Nashville, and

Charlotte. I want to immerse myself in the culture, without judgment and without preconceived notions."

"Ahh, kind of a gorillas in the mist kinda thing—or more like rednecks in the mess? You writing a book? Lemme guess—*Gone with the Fried Green Crawdads*? Folks do love *fictional* Southerners. Real ones are more boring. I know I am." He looked confused, so I cut him some slack and left him to his thoughts...or regrets. "Anyway, let me know if there's anything I can do to help. And seriously, if you hear a splash in the pool—"

"Stay away," he finished.

"Unless you're not disturbed enough already."

"I'm good," he assured me.

"For now. Give it time, kid."

"I've got a month and a half."

"One month down here, and you'll need therapy."

"That much going on here, huh?" he asked.

"Just the opposite. You're smack dab in the middle of the most boring spot on the planet. I'm OK with it, but it can drive some folks crazy—or drive them away."

"Well, now that I'm here," he said with a sly smile, "maybe it'll get more interesting."

"That's a pretty low bar. Not like it can get *less* interesting, but give it a shot, wild man."

"You seem a little disparaging about the place," Jack said. "I kind of had you pictured as a Southern—"

"Redneck? Hillbilly? Dumbass?"

"No, just somebody who loves the South. Like, really *really* loves the South."

"I did. Some of it, still do."

"Can you be more specific?"

"I could—if I felt like it. But I don't."

"OK."

"You're down here to learn about the South, right?" He nodded. "Let's see what you think after a few weeks—without me clouding your judgment, especially since I'm kind of an outcast in my own neck of the woods. I do want to know what *you* think, though, for real. Once you strip away the politics, the food, the accents, the scenery, it may not be as different as you think. People suck in Georgia. They suck in New York. They suck everywhere."

"How do you know if you haven't—"

"Believe me, kid. I *know*. I'll tell you about it sometime when I'm feeling, um, what's the word?"

"Candid? Garrulous?"

"No, *drunk*. Yeah, that's it. *That* would be the time for an interview. I'll reveal the secrets of the *yupneck*."

"And hopefully you'll explain what a *yupneck* is?"

"Half-yuppie, half-redneck. Well, maybe sixty percent redneck and half-yuppie."

"That doesn't add up," he said.

"It's new math. Speaking of new math, it's half past my bedtime."

"It's three o'clock in the afternoon."

"OK, an *hour* past. Nighty-night Hemingway."

* * *

The whirring of a blender and the sounds of my late idol Jimmy Buffett having no idea where he was a-gonna go in case of a volcanic eruption stirred Jack from his quarters. Yes, I'm a Parrot Head with a pool instead of a beach, pines instead of palms, and a wannabe creek instead of a sea. Buffett had ships and seaplanes, and I've got a silver Tacoma pickup and graffiti-decorated trains rolling through every couple of hours on the tracks behind my property, less than a quarter-mile from the house. Occasionally, I still crossed the three creosote-reeking railroad ties bound together that served as my family's old makeshift bridge across a narrow section of Boggy Branch to visit the tracks, just as I did growing up. It reminded me that life kept chugging along even when it felt stagnant. They sped almost violently through Possum Holler's woods. From the house, though, the noise was more sound-machine-like clickety-clacks providing percussion for the cicadas' nightly songs. It's definitely not a tropical paradise, but I needed the occasional pitcher of medicinal margaritas, especially on Sundays when most local folks were dutifully in their houses of worship—sometimes *twice* in the same day.

"Are you decent?" Jack asked as he approached my back deck, semi-shaded by a pergola tangled in overgrown honeysuckle.

"Above average, I reckon," I said.

My favorite ragged Georgia Bulldogs beach towel was draped over my shoulders like a cape. I was the self-crowned King of Possum Holler. My subjects were squirrels, deer, raccoons, and, yes, opossums with an *o*. (Calling the area *Opossum* Holler would be weird.) Much to Jack's relief, I imagine, I was no longer naked. I was dry and wearing blue Atlanta Braves lounging shorts.

"Thought I heard a blender," Jack said. "I could go for a smoothie."

"You *could* go for a smoothie," I said as I pointed south. "Might find one in Americus, about twelve miles yonder way."

"I take it that's not a virgin drink in the blender?" he asked.

"Kid, I haven't had a virgin *anything* in thirty years."

"Here you go, Uncle Ben."

The first words Jack Settles ever heard from my nephew came as JD handed me my insulated metal cup with the University of Georgia's G logo. I hated when he called me Uncle Ben because it conjured up images of the old black man in the chef's hat and made me crave rice. I only bought Mahatma out of spite. JD was about the same height as Jack but with a more athletic frame, and his dark hair was closely cropped. My hair was closely cropped, as well, but only because it helped make its gradual disappearance less dramatic. It's not that I cared what people thought, but I was forced to occasionally see my reflection in the mirror, and it was not a pleasant experience. JD had more enviable reasons to keep his hair short—so that it wouldn't bother him under his helmet as a strong safety in the fall and a third baseman in the spring.

"JD, this is the carpetbagger in the guest house—Jack Settles, or *John* for short," I said as I took a huge swig of my tropical treat. I usually nursed my weekend drinks as the sun set, but the heat spurred me to chug it like a frat boy on this day. And, like a twelve-year-old guzzling Slurpees from the 7-Eleven, it was totally worth the brain freeze.

"John is short for Jack?" JD asked as he glanced at his hand and appeared to count the letters on his fingers.

"I rest my case," I said with a told-you-so glance in Jack's direction. Jack seemed startled. I figured it was because I had told him that I lived alone and was not expecting anyone to be in my house, much less someone a similar age.

JD set his beer bottle on the rusty iron-grated homemade coffee table in front of his Adirondack chair and extended his hand. Jack winced as they shook.

"Welcome to God's country, Jack," JD said as he plopped down next to me and took a swig from his Tropicália. I allowed him to drink at my house, but only one beer if he was driving. I realize that doesn't qualify me for the Nobel Prize for Uncles but Georgia law requires each family to have one black sheep uncle who corrupts his nephews. JD was my *only* nephew, so I kept the corruption light. Besides, I think he viewed his visits to my house less as a free pass to misbehave and more of a wellness check on me. "I hope Uncle Ben ain't giving you too much of a hard time."

I could tell that Jack was also taken aback that JD's attire was so similar to his own—khaki pants, button-down blue shirt, and casual leather shoes. It was quite the contrast to my lounging shorts and flip-flops. These were *his* Sunday/go-to-meeting clothes. His dad, my brother-in-law, was the preacher at Riverside Free Will Church, which I dubbed Riverside "Free Pass" Church as most of its flock thumped their Bibles for excuses to hate various groups and weren't much into all that lovey-dovey Jesus stuff.

"No, he's been perfectly hospitable," Jack said, attempting to not offend me.

"You must've said perfectly *hostile*," JD argued with a chuckle. "Sorry, I don't hear so great out of my right ear."

"How long's that been going on, JD?" I asked, already knowing the answer.

"About 18 years now," he said. "Don't worry, Jack. You don't need sign language. I can hear well enough."

"*You* hear what you *want* to hear," I argued.

"Don't we all?" Jack interjected.

"Don't we all *what*?" I asked, wide-eyed at the gall of this newcomer trying to school us.

"Hear what we want to hear, see what we want to see?" Jack continued.

"I don't know, Sigmund, but last night a log truck jake-braking on the highway out there woke me up," I said. "I damn sure didn't *want* to hear that."

"It was probably just one of your farts," JD interrupted with a smile. "Was it a margarita night last night, too? Might wanna scale it back."

"It's medicinal," I said. "Doctor's orders."

"Who? Doctor Feelgood?"

"Scholl," I said. "Pepper Scholl. I don't think he accepts your Jesus insurance."

"He board certified?"

"I'm certifiably bored."

"Well, you're certifiable anyway."

"I take back my thoughts and prayers for you and your stupid ear," I said.

"You don't pray," he argued.

"Sorry," Jack said. "I didn't mean to start anything."

"Dude, you gotta lighten up," I said. "That's the way guys show affection down here."

"Aww, you love me," JD said.

"I *tolerate* you," I said.

"I'm sorry," JD said. "I didn't hear you."

If Jack had known at the time how little of a crap I gave about the world at that point in my life, offending me would have been of no concern. I'd lost a wife to divorce, a daughter to unrealistic fantasies, and a job in The Big Apple because I inherited this home and twenty-two acres in the boonies. I'd even lost my last dog, a black lab named Beau who wandered into the woods one night and never returned. Fortunately, my truck was still in the driveway, keeping my life from being a country music song—the old-school kind, not the modern mud-beer-flag-smalltown formulaic crap.

"You've got to watch him," JD continued. "He's not just full of tequila—he's also full of crap."

"Hey!" I admonished. "This is my first one. I ain't full of nothing—yet. And if you don't like it around here, you're welcome to chill out over at that prude Sarah Davis' house! See if she'll let you drink on the sabbath. Don't forget, just that one drink. You've got to be on your A game tomorrow."

"Sarah your girlfriend?" Jack asked as he sat down in the back porch swing. (Front porch swings are for people who like to visit. I still had a front porch swing but never used it. I'd have taken it down, but that could involve manual labor.) His innocent question made me spit out a precious mouthful of margarita.

"Actually, it's my mom," JD said with a smile.

"Yeah, if this were Alabama, maybe, but we don't do that kind of stuff in Georgia," I said as I tried to fake my serious face once again.

"Uncle Ben and my mom are brother and sister," JD explained. "And they pretty much hate each other."

"How's that?" Jack asked.

"Well, for one, my mom's at home cooking dinner after going to church for the second time today," JD said. "Uncle Ben's having margaritas for dinner and would burst into flames if he set foot in church."

"Hey, the G on this cup is for God," I countered.

"Bull!" JD responded.

"There ain't no bulls out here," I said facetiously. "I don't even have cows."

"The reason he dresses like he does all the time is just in case he up and dies because it's probably real hot where he's going," JD told Jack.

"Wait, back in January, you said it was cold as Hell. You church people need to get your stories straight. I'm starting to suspect it's all a fraud."

"Hey, I may not be quite as religious as Mom and Dad, but I'm still on the team," JD argued.

"The *pope* is not as religious as your mom and dad," I contended.

"I don't believe *everything* they believe," he said. "For instance, Jack, I believe in evolution, but I believe God did it."

"You trying to play on both sides?" I asked. "Does your mama know about this heresy?"

"No, it's easier to lie and pretend to agree with everything they say," he said.

"Ain't bearing false witness a sin?" I pressed.

"A minor one—unlike you, I try to keep my sins manageable," he said with a smile directed at Jack. "I've cut way back on murder and stuff. Besides, I'm at church every Sunday morning and Wednesday nights. That offsets minor sinning."

"I'd rather laugh with the sinners than cry with the saints...or go to that goddamn church," I said with a raise of my cup. "You only go because your dad's the preacher."

"I like to cover my bases. There are some good Christian folks at our church. They're not all hypocrites like you say."

"My atheist friends—"

"I thought you didn't have any friends?"

"My atheist *acquaintances* agree with Jesus more than your Christian folks. They actually do Jesus-y stuff—like helping the poor and stuff."

"I'll have you know we've got a mission team going to Guatemala next week," JD retorted.

"Yeah, to go hug on orphans, throw 'em some toys and bolt," I retorted.

"What are they supposed to do?"

"Oh, I don't know—build a house, do medical treatments, dig wells, stuff like that. I got a couple of atheist do-gooders I can hook your church folks up with—you know, if they're not offended by doing stuff Jesus purportedly gave a shit about."

"You sure that's your first drink?" Jack interrupted.

"First one, no lie," I said as I raised my cup again. "I ain't no lying sinner. I'm an honest-to-god sinner—so to speak."

"I'm afraid Uncle Ben has lost faith in the Lord, people, the nation, damn near everything, even himself. If you don't have faith in anything else, you've at least got to have faith in yourself."

"Did you read that in the Old or New Testament?" I asked.

"Panda Express, actually," he said. "Fortune cookie."

"Mmm, pandas," I said.

"In case you haven't noticed, Uncle Ben likes to stir up crap and try to get under your skin," JD told Jack. "You gotta take his bullshit with a grain of salt—or a rim of salt in his case. You know how some folks say they don't care what anybody thinks, yet they really do?"

"Yeah."

"Well, he's the guy who, for real, doesn't care what anybody thinks—at least, not anymore. Not so long ago, he was a normal human being."

"Amen!" I said. "JD here goes with the flow, never making any waves. Never gets in trouble. Everybody loves JD. He's apple pie, Jesus, the flag, and baseball. But he's got that Christian guilt that follows him everywhere."

"Guilt about what?" JD retorted.

"All the little sins—cussing, gluttony, pride, wearing clothes made of two different threads, drinking. I don't know how you're going to handle it if you ever commit one of those major sins."

"Maybe somewhere between never giving a shit and *always* giving a shit is just the right amount of shit," Jack chimed in.

"Oh really, Mr. Boston, and where do you stand between giving a shit and not giving a shit?" I asked.

"I'm not sure yet. I guess I'm a floater."

"Eww." JD recoiled at the thought before laughing.

"But that's what this whole trip's about—trying to figure out what's real, what's not, what's important...you know, stuff like that."

"He's writing a book, JD—*Gone with the Fried Green Crawdads*," I explained. "Be careful what you say around him. He's taking mental notes. He's gonna make us look even crazier than we are."

"I *am* keeping a journal," Jack admitted, "but no book. And I have no idea what a crawdad is."

"Jesus Christ!" I exclaimed with a facepalm.

"A journal?" JD asked bewilderedly. "I didn't know people still *wrote*...on purpose anyway."

"Yeah," I chimed in. "Poor kid doesn't know that he could jot down every interesting thing about Possum Holler on a Post-It. Post-Its are rarely best-sellers, by the way."

"Hey, whose is that?" Jack asked as he nodded toward the back door, where my blue guitar was leaning against the wall. I bought it when I was in college. It made Rhode Island feel warmer because the face was painted with a beach scene—a couple of palm trees, sand, beach ball, and waves. The only thing that irked me was that it bore the words "Lifes a beach." I was a numbers guy, but that missing apostrophe bugged me.

"It's his," JD said. "My Dad taught me some chords, and Uncle Ben taught me a few Buffett songs. Now, I'm almost as bad as he is."

"You're welcome," I said. "You play any instruments, Jack? Harp? Flute? Piccolo?"

"Actually, believe it or not, I have a Yamaha my dad handed down to me when I turned twelve. I think he only gave it to me as an excuse to buy himself some fancy Martin with a mahogany neck."

"You play?" I asked. "Feel free to grab mine and give us your best Jerry Reed impression."

"I don't know who Jerry Reed is, but—"

"WHAT?!" I yelled in faux outrage. "You've seen *Smokey and the Bandit*, right? Snowman? I swear he deserved an Oscar for Best Supporting Actor. Him or Fred."

"I've *heard* of *Smokey and the Bandit*, yes," he said.

"Oh my God," I said with a facepalm. "You've got a lot to learn. Well, play something. Anything."

"Nope," Jack said. "If you think you two are bad—"

"It's 'y'all,' not 'you two'," I corrected.

"Sorry, if *y'all* think *y'all* are bad guitar players, *y'all* ain't seen nothin' yet."

"Well, I'll be damned. That's the first thing you've said that I totally understood."

"Here's to bad guitar players!" JD raised his beer for another toast, and Jack reached into his shirt pocket.

"Watch it, JD," I said. "He's pulling a weapon. You know how that Northern gun culture is!"

"It's a vape pen," Jack said. "I don't really drink. Kinda hurts my tummy, you know."

"Your what?" I asked.

"My vape pen."

"No, that thing that hurts sometimes."

"My tummy?"

"Jesus, you *need* a drink," I said as I grabbed my pitcher and poured a Solo cup half-full.

"Seriously," Jack said, "I would drink a virgin margarita."

"Don't worry," I said. "When *you* drink it, it *is* a virgin margarita."

"What makes you think that?" he asked.

"Well, the use of the word *tummy* for one," I said as I handed him the drink. "JD can help you fix that this summer. He's been out with half the girls between here and Americus. And if that don't work, they've got sheep over at the Miller place down the road."

"He's joking, right?" Jack asked JD.

"Well, I have dated a few girls, but they were all better as just friends. I'm in no hurry. I'm not old like Uncle Ben. And, yeah, they really do have sheep down at the Miller place," JD said. "But, no, I don't think Uncle Ben's serious about the wooly-bully stuff."

"Night's still young," I said with a tip of my cup. "And stop calling me Uncle Ben. You know I prefer Your Highness when you're over here."

"Your Highness?" Jack pressed.

"Yeah," JD responded. "He's not just the king of bullshit; he's the King of Possum Holler!"

"Where's that?"

"You're smack dab in the middle of my kingdom, kid, right here on the Macon County-Sumter County line," I interjected.

"Well," Jack said with another raise of his beer, "all hail the King!" We each took a swig and looked toward the sun, which was beginning its descent into the woods behind the house. "It's really a beautiful kingdom. You grow up here?"

"Yeah, well until I ran off with a band," I said. "Ever heard of a band called Starbuck? 'Moonlight Feels Right'?"

"I've heard of their coffee," Jack said as he shook his head.

"I was the xylophonist. Got the big head and set out solo."

"A *solo* xylophonist?" Jack asked while JD looked down at his sweating beer and grinned.

"Yeah, didn't work out as well as you might think."

"Bullshit?" Jack asked JD, who nodded.

"You really need some more modern pop culture references," JD said. "I'm pretty sure you were about five when that song came out."

"I was a child prodigy, dammit!"

"Seriously," Jack interjected. "What's your real story, besides ruling over Possum Holler?"

I lay back in my chair and cracked my knuckles. JD knew and Jack would come to learn that this was my unconscious signal that it was time for a bullshit break.

"I don't have a 'story' for your quote-unquote research, but I did have a bit of a winding road out of Possum Holler—and *back.*"

I explained I was indeed a prodigy—albeit in math, not music. Though my current slob appearance and living situation might have hinted otherwise, I was once a straight-laced Ivy Leaguer, the first and only one from Possum Holler as far as I know. I got a Master of Finance from Brown University in Providence, Rhode Island, because I was a numbers whiz, and it seemed like a safe foundation for a financially rewarding career, which is what my folks wanted. That was back when I was easily steered and influenced. I got my minor in history, though I had no plans for it at the time other than bolstering my chances on *Jeopardy* someday. Unlike math, history *fascinated* me, perhaps because in grade school we spent too much time on Phoenicians and ancient Greeks and always wound up breezing through the most recent 200 years, the ones I considered more relevant, in a couple of weeks as time ran out before summer break. As a teenager, I started to wonder if the Vietnam War was an urban legend because never did a teacher ever get around to it. One college course devoted exclusively to the Civil War particularly piqued my interest as I began to see how repulsive the motivations of the South truly were. It was the first major blow to the Southern pride with which most Georgia schoolkids had been indoctrinated in the seventies.

Sure enough, I landed a well-paying boring gig as a financial analyst on Wall Street and bought a simple flat in Brooklyn before the area got too hipster and pricey. Life was progressing according to an excruciatingly dull plan. I'd escaped podunk Possum Holler and established myself as a cool New York City cat. However, when *everyone's* cool, no one's cool. I was just a marching ant in a Big Apple full of them. The only people impressed with my so-called success were my folks back home.

I met Elizabeth at a jazz club in downtown Manhattan, though I barely knew jazz from Starbuck or Lynyrd Skynyrd at that point. I was nursing an Old Fashioned at the bar with my tie loosened when she straddled up next to me to get the bartender's attention. I had no joy in my life and no purpose, but I was not aware how much the light had left my eyes. I was merely existing and not sure why I bothered to do so. But I must have looked downright depressed compared to the other jovial patrons because I felt her intensely staring at me with those dark, soulful eyes. Her black curls bounced with every move of her head as she ordered two cosmopolitans and leaned against the bar with her smooth bare arms extended from a multi-colored bohemian dress that made her stand out like a mermaid in a sea of tie-wearing cod.

"You OK?" she asked as she leaned unapologetically into my personal space. Her British accent caught me off-guard. Even at Brown and at work, I had met very few people with British accents. And having grown up in Possum Holler, I did not have much experience bantering with black girls. It was frowned upon where I grew up, especially back in the days when I still gave a crap what people thought. I grew up an accepted conformist in Possum Holler before I made the unimpressive leap to become an invisible conformist in The Big Apple. I could barely recognize either of those conformists today.

"Oh, sorry," I said nervously. "I look like some stereotypical drunk at the bar, huh? I'm just totally worn out from work stuff. First drink actually."

"What do you do?" she asked.

"Financial analyst at—"

"Sounds horrible," she interrupted.

"Nah, it's merely awful," I said with a half-smile. "How about you?"

"Actress. Singer. Artist."

"Wow, that's impressive."

"Yeah, failing at all three. I might try failing as a dancer next."

"You should try modeling," I blurted out to my embarrassment, realizing too late that I had vocalized what I was thinking. She smiled with no inkling of embarrassment. "I mean, you know, just keeping with the artsy kind of stuff. I didn't mean because you're pretty."

"Aww, you think I'm pretty," she practically sang in a sultry tone.

"That's not what I meant. I mean, yes, you are, um, gorgeous, but I didn't mean to *say* that. Out loud. That was inappropriate. I'm sorry. I'm gonna drown myself in this drink now."

"It's only inappropriate if it's *un*wanted," she said while refusing to break eye contact.

"Hey, I'm totally on board with the whole no means no thing," I stammered.

"Good boy. But, *sometimes*, yes means yes." She grabbed a napkin off the bar and began writing. "I'm Elizabeth. This is my number. Call me *sometime*...or tomorrow night, and let's talk about when you're gonna take me out. I'm thinking Thursday. There's a show at The Artists' Space in Soho I wanna see, and Tiffany over there can't join me."

"I'm Benjamin, well, Ben. Um, Tiffany? Is she—"

"My roommate. She's not my girlfriend if that's what you're scared to ask. At least, not usually." She grabbed the two cosmos as soon as the bartender placed them upon the bar. "Lucky for you, I'm available...for the moment. Don't dawdle. Talk to you tomorrow, Benjamin!"

"Ben," I corrected. "Benjamin means I'm in trouble."

"Still might be," she said with a wink. She delivered the round of drinks to the two-person table she shared with Tiffany, and they jumped right back into a conversation without so much as glancing my way. I figured it was routine for her to flirt and hand out her phone number. I genuinely was just out to wind down, not to carouse. That whirlwind encounter gave me whiplash. It was a Tuesday, after all, and rarely did I do anything besides work or sleep on a weeknight. I had just endured an unusually aggravating day at the office. Yet, this bold, brash, artsy, beautiful girl intrigued me. Maybe she was what I needed to shake me out of the doldrums, I thought. I needed something *different*. All the sameness around me in New York was likely of my own choices, yet it was beginning to suffocate me.

The next day I told my nearest co-worker Josh that I was going on a Thursday night date.

"You're getting laid on a weeknight? Damn, and I thought I knew you!"

"No, no, no," I corrected him. "This girl is different. Don't get me wrong—she's hot. Way the heck out of my league, in fact. But we talked for an hour on the phone last night."

"Dude, you haven't spoken an hour's worth of words to *anyone* since you've been here," he said.

"I know. That's what I mean. She's interesting."

"And I'm not?" he asked, half-jokingly.

"Not particularly."

"Damn, coming from the most boring guy in New York City, that's pretty brutal."

"Don't worry—what you lack in personality, you make up for with a lack of production."

"Anybody ever tell you you're a little too honest?"

"Lying is a sin."

"Well, take a little advice from a guy who actually has a life and goes out with, you know, actual women: Don't be *too* honest with this new chick. They like a little mystery."

"Too late," I said. "I told her my whole life story last night. Honestly."

"And you talked for an hour?"

"Yeah," I said.

"What did you talk about for the other 55 minutes?"

I waved him off and got back to work. He had a valid point. I was not even remotely intriguing. She was *fascinating*. She grew up in Southwark—South London—the only daughter of a South African father and a Nigerian mother. She studied Contemporary Art Theory at the University of Edinburgh but got bored with the program and felt trapped in the "tiny" city of more than a half-million. She vowed to never be stuck in a tiny town ever again and headed across the pond to The Big Apple. The only thing I hid from her were the words "Possum Holler." I merely told her I was from a rural area of Georgia. The word Possum alone could have gotten our date canceled.

It was the greatest first date of my life. We hit the art show, and she gushed about works while I nodded with as much interest and understanding as I would have had at an exhibition of owner's manuals for refrigerators. Seeing her eyes light up at each stop, however, was all the show I needed. She *was* the artwork. When she suggested we grab wings and nachos at O'Keefe's in Brooklyn Heights because they were showing the Rangers game, I wondered if I was being punked. Then I remembered they only punked folks people gave a shit about or had at least heard of. She yelled and high-fived guys at the table closest to us all three times the Rangers scored a goal on their way to a 3-0 lead over the Capitals after one period. I wasn't a hockey fan just yet because I thought the scores were too rare compared to football. Compared to Premier League soccer, however, I guess hockey was nonstop action.

"We've got this," she said. "How 'bout we go to my flat for a nightcap?"

* * *

I sighed aloud as I paused the story.

"You all right?" Jack asked.

"Yeah, yeah."

"Is this bullshit, too?"

"Is *what* bullshit?"

"The whole New York City, Ivy Leaguer, business guy, boy meets girl, yadda yadda yadda."

"No. We got married. She did her artsy stuff, while I made money—mainly for other folks. Had a nice home in Brooklyn, the Williamsburg area before it became trendy. Then Riley

Savannah came along. We were living the quintessential New York City life. "

"What happened?" Jack asked.

"Elizabeth was a different woman from one day to the next, which kept things interesting. But the city was the same damn place, day after day. Everybody seemed so two-dimensional, and I was the worst example of it. Going through the daily motions, spinning my wheels. Just another boring face in the crowd, another suit and tie in Manhattan during the day, and another worn-out yuppie on the weekend. Then Daddy died."

"That's how he went from The Big Apple to The Big Possum," JD interjected.

"Massive heart attack," I continued. "Mama died of cancer just a couple months before that, and JD's mom had to take care of both of them in those final months."

"You mean your *sister*," JD interjected.

"Whatever. Anyway, they guilted me about being up in New York and convinced me that Riley would be better off in a small town than in the big city. She was eight at the time, and I thought if Possum Holler could turn out a human being as wonderful as me, maybe it could do the same for her. I got the house and twenty-two acres and decided to make it our own little country paradise. Online trading had become a thing, so I could make my own money and do less work. Elizabeth could have this perfect little art studio in the country, and Riley would be surrounded by fresh air, family, and nature, plenty of room to grow and thrive. I had purpose. I had joy. I thought life was good."

"Sounds like a great plan," Jack said.

"Does, don't it. Then it all went to hell," I said.

"I thought you didn't believe in hell," JD argued.

"Well, it sure as hell didn't turn out to be heaven like I'd imagined. Make yourself useful and get me another drink. I'm depressing myself. And you need to wrap it up. You've got a big game tomorrow."

"What kind of game?" Jack asked.

"Baseball," JD said simply.

"Only the damn state championship," I clarified to Jack. "You know, that game you've been preparing for since travel ball started turning eight-year-olds into pros instead of kids."

"I thought school was out," Jack asked.

"It is," I explained, "but a few rainouts messed up the schedule and delayed the state playoffs. Hell, JD graduated on Friday. Most of his classmates are already on their senior trips to the Redneck Riviera—well, except for a couple of other guys on the team anyway."

"Hey, I'm heading to Panama City as soon as the game's over, win or lose. You should come, Jack," JD suggested, prompting a momentary look of confusion from my guest. "I mean to the game, not PC."

"It's not like I've got a whole lot of plans," Jack said. "Where and when?"

"3 p.m., Muckalee Christian. Winner-take-all Game 3. Uncle Ben—er, forgive me, I mean the *King*—can tell you where. He's a history teacher there."

"Wait," Jack said. "You, mister atheist, devout follower of the messiah of margaritas, teach at a *Christian* private school?"

"Yep. I'm their dose of reality, especially when it comes to history. After all, nobody even makes the connection that all these so-called Christian schools around here were founded in 1965, '66, '67—coincidentally, of course, the same time all the public schools around here got desegregated. I guess Jesus helped them *re*-segregate in private. Besides, I wanted Riley to go there."

"You don't feel like a hypocrite?"

"Everybody's at least a little bit of a hypocrite in one way or another. Besides, for all I don't like about private schools, they have more freedom and less red tape than public schools, and I wanted Riley to get the best education she could. And, I teach *actual* history, not *Christian* history. They can go to church and be spoon-fed whether what happened in the past was right or wrong, but their preachers and parents can't *change* history. They can overlook inconvenient parts of history, like they do with the Bible, but they can't *change* it. Besides, I needed to get out of the house because I felt like my being at home all the time was smothering Elizabeth. Besides, when it comes to Jesus, He and I are on the same team. He wasn't much into religion, either."

"The atheist team? How's that?" Jack probed further.

"I doubt *their* Jesus needs all the worship and confirmation they believe in him. He probably knows whether he exists or not. I think he'd rather be on the side of the people who are more in line with his teachings and beliefs—you know, be nice to folks, the Beatitudes, and stuff. When it comes to that, I'm way more Christian than most American Christians. You won't catch them trying to post the Beatitudes in courthouses and classrooms, only the Ten Commandments."

"I just hope Jesus is on *our* side tomorrow," JD said as he stood and slapped me on the back and extended his hand to Jack. "Nice meeting you, Jack. Hope you can make the game. If not, I'm sure I'll be seeing you around the *kingdom* this summer. Hope you find something interesting to put in your book."

"Oh, I have no doubt now," Jack said in a tone that seemed unusually definitive. "This is just day one. I may need a whole stack of Post-Its before it's all said and done."

"Clearly, you ain't from around here," I said. "Nothing ever happens around here, and there's been a whole lot more *nothing* lately than usual. Most folks can't handle it."

"How do *you* handle it?" Jack asked.

"This little slice of nothing's all I've got left, kid. And if it's all I've got, I might as well wallow in it. All this beautiful, oppressive nothing—all goddamn twenty-two acres of it."

Jack smirked before walking back to the guest house.

"What?" I asked.

"Nothing, but I think I'm gonna need more colorful Post-Its. Yellow's not gonna cut it for this project."

"Why do I feel like I'm going to be a lead character in *Gone with the Fried Green Crawdads?*"

"I told you: It's just a journal full of notes," he reminded me. "Although, *The King of Possum Holler* has a nice ring to it for a book title."

I was starting to like this skinny Yankee kid. I hoped I wouldn't regret it.

# Chin Music

I was surprised that Jack *wanted* to go to the championship game. I thought he was just trying to be polite to JD as the previous day's invite came out of the blue. However, Jack was bouncing with excitement in the driveway beside my truck when I exited the house. He was wearing a Boston Red Sox hat and a generic red Nike shirt with athletic shorts and sneakers. He looked semi-normal, albeit more like a twelve-year-old kid bound for Fenway Park than an eighteen-year-old college student headed to see a bunch of kids he didn't know play on a rural diamond behind Muckalee Christian School. I'm pretty sure that was not on his summer itinerary a couple of days earlier.

"You sure you wanna go?" I asked him as I hopped into the driver's side. "It's only 98 degrees with 112 percent humidity. JD won't be offended. He'll probably be so focused on the game that he won't even notice I'm there until it's over."

"Never too hot for a baseball game," he said.

"We're gonna test that theory today," I said. "You play?"

"I did until I was about twelve."

"What happened?"

"Not much. I sucked."

"I'm surprised the Red Sox didn't draft you then," I said with my usual straight face, which had three days' worth of beard grown since Friday's graduation ceremony. I planned to shave the morning after the championship when the teachers would return to do our annual summer break classroom straightening up without the students.

The stands on the home team's first-base side were packed with too many familiar faces. I didn't want to squeeze in and feel shoulders rubbing mine or knees in my back—or, worse, have home fans give me tinnitus as they bitched about every umpire's call that went against us. Unlike the Muckalee Christian alums and parents, I could be semi-objective—so long as JD got *his* fair share of calls anyway.

Besides, the home stands were a little too white for this white boy, as in one hundred percent white. Don't get me wrong—some of my best friends are white—just not *that* white. I'm kidding, of course. As JD had noted the day before, I didn't have any true friends—by choice, theirs and mine.

The visiting stands, however, had a sprinkling of black people, including a couple that appeared to be a husband and wife. Our Muckalee Christian Academy Mudcats were hosting St. Barnabas Catholic School from Columbus, a little more than an hour from Americus. There is a caveat to what I implied when telling Jack about many "Christian" schools being formed across the South during the early years of desegregation. Many of the Catholic schools in the state seemed to be genuinely founded for religious reasons and often had diverse student populations. It was as if they actually believed that Jesus stuff about loving *everybody*, even the non-white—like Jesus himself. Still, this wasn't just baseball—a sport drawing fewer black athletes across the board each year—but it was *private school* baseball, so the sight of non-white folks in Muckalee's stands was rare. I scanned the field and could barely make out that one of the Hurricanes—yes, St. Barnabas adopted the name "Hurricanes" even though they were three hours from the Gulf Coast—was a short black kid making soft warm-up tosses with teammates in left field.

I scoped out a spot just beyond the Mudcats' dugout near the makeshift bullpen where our star senior pitcher, Fletcher "Fletch" Thomas was warming up with our star senior catcher, Doug "DC" Cassel. Each of them was expected to be drafted by Major League teams in a few weeks, though probably not high enough for them to eschew their full-ride scholarships at Mercer University. I'd taught each of them American and World History, and I was genuinely happy to see them have a future on the diamond after this contest. They weren't the smartest kids I'd ever taught, but baseball had given them an opportunity to further their education. They wouldn't be able to attend a school like Mercer otherwise. Because JD considered them friends, I had faith they might even turn out to be decent adults. Fletch's parents kept an RV in a park across The Strip from the Gulf of Mexico on the east end of Panama City Beach where JD, DC, and Fletch were planning to go the next morning—hopefully as state champs. They also had to know how close JD had been with Riley during her freshman and sophomore years at Muckalee. If JD considered those boys friends, I assumed they weren't as prejudiced as their parents nor as racist as their grandparents. Perhaps they were part of a transformational generation more in touch with the future than the past.

"I'm gonna make a concession stand run," I told Jack. "You want a beer?"

"What?"

"Geez. I'm kidding. You're gonna need to get a little faster to keep up. How 'bout a Diet Coke?"

"Regular Coke, please."

"OK, one Diet Coke for me and one liquid diabetes for you."

Condensation ran down the cup and over my fingers by the time I got back to Jack and the bag chairs he had opened for us. His face was pale, even by his standards.

"Here," I said as I handed him his carbonated poison. "You all right? You look like you've seen a ghost."

"Yeah, the ghost of Jim Crow."

"What are you talking about?"

"Those guys who were just warming up—I swear the catcher told him, 'Hit the brother.' And the pitcher nodded and smiled."

"Nah," I reassured him. "I mean, yeah, most of the grandparents here long for the days when there were whites-only water fountains, and I'm sure there are still plenty of prejudiced kids here, especially the more elite ones—you know, the kinds who preface racist comments by saying, 'You know, I'm not racist, but...' as if it makes whatever they're about to say OK. Fletch and DC are farm boys. They're not pampered. They're from working folks. Besides, I've never heard them say anything racist. And this is the state championship. I mean, it's private school ball, and there's only like eighteen schools in the whole damn classification, but it's still a state title on the line. It'd be pretty stupid to hit a batter on purpose and put them on base."

"Hope you're right."

Dorothy Hall, the school's volunteer chorus director, then stepped onto the mound. "Don't let her fool you," I warned Jack with a nudge. "She may look old, but she's got a hell of a fastball."

Dorothy—or "Dot," as we all knew her—had been performing the National Anthem at Muckalee Christian baseball games for at least thirty years. She was also the music director at Muckalee Baptist Church and thought she was the second coming of Maria Callas. Though her voice had faded in recent years, the home crowd always applauded her as if Maria herself had beamed down from Heaven to perform. I found her renditions adequate, though I was convinced she sang "by the dawn's *swirly* light" each time. Perhaps it was a speech impediment. I don't know if light gets *swirly*, but if it does, it's probably closer to sunset than to dawn. When she finished, I put my Braves cap back on and politely clapped for whatever period of time seemed patriotic enough. Jack followed my lead and we sat back down.

"Not a fan of the song?" Jack asked.

"No, it's a great song. Got a good beat. You can dance to it. I'd give it a seventy-nine—eighty-plus if they sing the third stanza."

"The one about the slaves who fought with the British and how we Americans stuck it to them?"

"Wow, you know your history," I noted. "That makes two of us here. Of course, it'd take five minutes to sing all four stanzas."

"You got a better idea for a national anthem?" he asked with a chuckle.

"'Margaritaville' or 'Shake Your Booty' or 'You Can Call Me Al' or 'Purple People Eater' or...I can go on."

"Please don't."

"'Gettin' Jiggy'—"

"Oh, God, make it stop!"

"Speaking of God, shh. The team's praying."

"Somebody get hurt already?" he asked earnestly.

"You're in the South, kid. Remember? We pray about all kinds of stuff. We ask the Lord to cure our folks' cancer and praise him if he does and thank him anyway if he calls them home. We pray for rain when it's dry and pray for the rain to stop when it's too much. And then we go on Facebook and ask for unspoken prayers with a note that God knows what it's about. And, of course, folks pray before they eat."

"I've seen some interesting food on the way down here," Jack said. "I totally get the praying. You don't, huh?"

"Only before chili. Gives me heartburn."

"I mean, do you pray at all?"

"I asked for Powerball numbers a few years ago," I said. "Still waiting."

"That tracks. What are *they* praying for?" he asked with a nod toward the still-huddled team.

"Usual stuff: Keep us safe. Help us play to the best of our ability. Help us embarrass the hell out of the other team. Then they'll point to the sky if they hit a home run because the Lord clearly helped them do that instead of stopping wars, curing cancer or bringing the rain. Of course, it doesn't work *both* ways. Nobody ever says, 'We'd have won if Jesus hadn't made me drop that fly ball.' Sweet gig being God—all the credit and none of the blame."

The team's "Amen!" was quickly followed by a "One, two, three, Mudcats!" and a whole bunch of butt-slaps, fist-pumps, and high-fives before they took the field.

"All right! Let's go!" I cheered. "Jesus is on our side!"

A few people in the stands glanced my way. They never seemed to know if I was serious or not. Dr. Robert Jenkins, the headmaster, gave me a dirty look and a disapproving shake of his head. He took over the headmaster's job a year earlier with the intention of "refocusing Muckalee Christian's attention on faith." He'd graduated from Muckalee about the same time I graduated from Macon County High School, though we didn't know each other then. Many of his old classmates believed that the school had become "too secular" over the past fifteen years that his uncle had run the school, a time during which the student body population had gone from zero black kids to twelve. Nine of those twelve were either football or basketball players or both. The school was no more secular than it had ever been, but right-wing Christians often perceive that if things change or even appear different, the world is on the verge of collapse. They figured they were about one long-haired male student away from having drag queen story hours replace daily devotions. So, Dr. Jenkins decided the school's new motto would be Rooted In Christ. He ordered the Ten Commandments be posted in every classroom. Because Muckalee Christian is a private school, he didn't need permission from the courts. His face turned blood red when he walked in my classroom and saw that I had not posted the Ten Commandments but Jesus' Beatitudes instead.

"Just trying to stay 'Rooted In Christ,' you know," I explained to him at the time, knowing how few of our local Christians were actual fans of the Beatitudes or any red letters in the Bible. They preferred the eye-for-an-eye Old Testament and its vengeful God, though they didn't spend much time preaching to adults about Noah's Ark and Jonah. They saved such ridiculousness for the children's Sunday school. They weren't anti-indoctrination; they were pro *their* indoctrination. If they hadn't started the school in the sixties to keep their white kids from having to learn with black kids, they'd have eventually gotten around to founding a Christian school anyway.

* * *

St. Barnabas went three up, three down in the top of the first. Fletch then helped his cause in the bottom of the first with a two-run bomb over the left-field fence. He continued cruising in the top of the second inning, striking out the first two batters. Then, the short black kid came up to bat. Fletch reared back with a sly grin and zipped a fastball right under the kid's chin, sending him stumbling out of the batter's box and into the dirt. The ump merely issued a quiet "ball" call. Our coach said nothing. Even the St. Barnabas fans were subdued, as if they had seen this kind of thing before. Fletch smirked as he got the ball back from a laughing DC and strolled to the back of the mound to revisit the rosin bag.

JD asked for time and jogged to the mound. Neither he nor Fletch covered his mouth as usual during such discussions. Their voices were whispers, but JD's expression was loud. They weren't discussing strategy, as I could tell from reading their lips.

"What the hell?" JD mumbled.

"It got away from me," Fletch responded.

"It's the dadgum state championship, man! Seriously."

Coach Martin set one foot onto the field and yelled, "Break it up! Let's go!"

JD slowly walked back to third, and the batter returned to the plate. His grip on the bat was a little looser, and his feet were dancing. It was a fastball again—this time right down the center of the plate for a strike, though the batter bailed almost as soon as Fletch released it. The kid hung in there on the next pitch, though, and nearly swung out of his shoes. It was a two-hopper that JD easily gloved before throwing him out at first. Fletch tried to tap JD's glove as they jogged back to the dugout with the third out, but he was rebuffed. I looked at Jack and shook my head in disappointment. It was plausible that the first fastball under the chin was an honest attempt to set the batter up for the next two pitches. If it was indeed just baseball, it worked. Fletch wouldn't be the first pitcher to brush back a batter to set up a fastball down the middle. But JD's disgust was a red flag.

Between innings, it was as if nothing had happened. There was no drama. JD would be the fourth man up in the inning and talked to no one in the dugout as he donned his batting gloves and grabbed his helmet. Our first two batters reached on singles before a double made it 3-0. JD then stepped to the plate and ripped the first pitch he saw against the fence in right-center. He took third with a triple as the center-fielder struggled to come up with it cleanly. It was 5-0 with nobody out. He would score on a wild pitch before the Hurricanes made a pitching change and ended the rally. After four innings, our boys led comfortably, 8-3. The black kid was due to lead off the fifth.

He stepped to the plate a little more confidently this time and took a couple of solid practice swings. Fletch nodded with approval of the first sign Doug flashed. A fastball whizzed up and in. The kid tried to dive out of the way, but the ball hit the end of his bat as he fell down yet again. The umpire yelled, "Strike!" Indeed, the ball hit the bat, making it a legitimate strike, but it also struck a nerve with JD.

My nephew had always been a go-along-to-get-along kind of kid, too much of a conformist in my book, much like my younger self. Yet, I was rapidly transitioning from a teacher who bit his lip to a sarcastic cynic with one of my few remaining joys in life being my recently discovered ability to rankle right-wingers, traditionalists, and the status quo. In the past few months leading up to graduation, JD had grown contemplative and was not hanging out with his buddies and blowing off steam as you'd expect of a popular senior. Something was gnawing at him, but I never asked him what. I figured he needed one person in his family who offered a safe space from expectations and judgment. He could tell me anything. But he never told me how close he was getting to "screw it all" mode, nor did he offer any hints of it in his visits to my kingdom. I just thought he was growing more serious with age. However, he was about to jump off the "screw it all" cliff more memorably than Elvis cliff-dived in *Fun in Acapulco*.

JD marched toward his friend on the mound again, but this time he passed inches from Fletch and muttered something under his breath while bumping Fletch with his elbow. He kept walking to the dugout, took off his glove, and calmly put it in his bag. He then grabbed his bag and kicked open the gate near us.

"I quit!" he told Coach Martin, who grabbed him by the back of his jersey.

"We're a couple of innings from the title, JD! Get your butt back on third!" JD wrestled out of his grip and stormed past me and Jack, head held down all the way, never looking up or at us. "Don't you want to be a champion?!"

JD stopped and looked Coach Martin directly in the eyes. "Not like this, Coach. Not like *them*."

I proudly stood, folded my chair, and began putting it matter-of-factly in its carry bag as if we had just witnessed the last out of the game. "I quit, too," I calmly said aloud for the benefit of Coach Martin and the players and fans within earshot. Jack nervously attempted to put his chair back in the bag amid the unfolding drama. "You've got it upside-down, kid," I said with a grin. "Don't you Yankees know anything?"

All eyes were focused our way, though more *through* us and toward JD, who kept walking. One glare, though, was reserved for me.

"I know you had something to do with this!"

It was Sarah, my sister, stomping JD's way with her righteous preacher husband.

"Jack, this is my sister Sarah and her husband, the Rev. Ronnie Davis." I introduced as if we had just bumped into them at the grocery store. Jack gave them an embarrassed nod.

"You make me sick!" she huffed before joining the pastor in pursuit of JD. "You've ruined everything!"

"We all have our gifts," I hollered to the back of her storming-off head with a smile. "By the way, I've never been prouder of JD!"

"Oh, I'm sure you are!" she yelled back.

Jack's mouth was agape. I tried to reassure him with a comforting smile, though I suspect he saw it as more of a Cheshire Cat grin. We looked back toward the stands, where all eyes were on us while Coach Martin assembled his team on the mound for a pep talk.

"You're enjoying this aren't you?" Jack asked.

"Oh, hell yeah. I bet you're gonna be able to fill a whole Post-It with this story."

"Where do you think you're going?"

The headmaster, Dr. Jenkins, slapped his fat hand on my shoulder from behind. Veins bulged from his bald, red forehead.

"Well," I told him, "I've gotta run by Piggly Wiggly and grab a couple of steaks and a twelve-pack before it gets too late. Need me to get you anything?"

"You're fired! You're not Muckalee Christian material!"

"I sure as hell hope not. But, hey, if you're OK with trying to injure a kid just because he's black, you *definitely* are Muckalee Christian material. Enjoy your tainted championship. And, hey, no hard feelings. I hope you win Most Valuable Racist."

"Get out of here!"

"Gladly, and may the good Lord give y'all everything you deserve. Adios, amigos!"

I waved my final goodbye to everyone and to the building where I'd been teaching for several years. I whispered to Jack as we were walking away, "By the way, that's Spanish for *goodbye, racist assholes*—I don't know if you've studied advanced Spanish."

"You're gonna get shot one day," he said.

"Been there, done that. Story for another day."

I'd come to the field to see some kids I liked, including JD, celebrate a state title. I didn't really care whether the school itself would add a 56th piece of hardware to their trophy case. Yet, I felt like a champion myself as we walked to the parking lot.

Personal victories had been hard to come by in recent years, and, dammit, I was going to enjoy this one.

Ahead of me, I saw JD's little blue Ford Ranger spin out of the parking lot and head right, followed closely by my sister and brother-in-law in their white Kia sedan. We followed about a half-mile behind them as we headed north along 49. JD passed Andersonville National Historic Site and kept going past the turn to their home in the Cutoff community. His parents gave up the pursuit and turned toward their house. At some point, he'd have to go home and face the music for letting down his teammates, school, and family—well, *immediate* family anyway.

He had already skipped the road to my house, where he probably figured he would get a slap on the back for taking a stand. Sure, I was proud of him, but I was not going to throw him a party for doing the right thing. He was growing into a decent young man, and I never doubted that he would have a set of respectable principles despite all the religious guilt and fear pumped into him by his parents, church, and school. Besides, because he was so close with his biracial cousin before she left for New York City, I knew that JD's actions on the diamond were not merely some stand against injustice. It was personal.

Riley was one year older than JD. I'd seen them swim and play together as kids before she developed a taste for The Big Apple during her later visits with Elizabeth. After her sophomore year at Muckalee, Riley bolted for New York City.

After a couple of years in New York, her resentment for me grew over my having brought them to Possum Holler in the first place. As a freshman at CCNY, she visited me one last time just before Christmas—mainly to inform me face to face that she was never coming back to Possum Holler. She said she hated everything about the home I had worked so hard to make perfect for Elizabeth and her. She hated the food. She hated the weather. She hated everybody in the state of Georgia—including me.

"JD is the only one in this whole damn state that I give a shit about!" Those words still echo in my head.

"So, that's why you converted the studio into a rental?" Jack asked after hearing the story.

"Yeah. Hey, do me a favor." I handed him my phone and cleared the lock screen as I pulled off the road and turned around in a field to head back to Possum Holler. "Text JD. Tell him to drop by for a minute before he goes home. I've got a plan."

"Should I be worried?" Jack asked as he began to type with his thumbs.

"Probably."

"Where's he going anyway?"

"He's probably down at Timber Creek under the railroad trestle—his so-called Thinking Spot. You can actually walk the tracks behind the house to get there, too. I used to do it all the time growing up. It's not even two miles from here. Guess he was in a hurry to do his thinking today."

"Mine's the Longfellow Bridge over the Charles," Jack said. "I suspect the trestles over the creek here are a little quieter."

"Well, until the trains come anyway," I said. "Whole damn thing shakes like an earthquake, horns blaring. Not exactly my idea of getting away from it all."

"Where's *your* spot?" he asked.

"Well, it *was* the house—the back deck, the pool, the woods, the branch. It was *my* paradise anyway, especially after New York. Now, it's just Paradise Lost, where all my dreams went to hell. The only way I get any peace now is when I get drunk and pretend I'm somewhere else."

"Like where?"

"You're about to find out," I said. "That's part of the plan."

"Oh yeah. And I should be worried?"

"Probably maybe but hardly definitely."

"That's reassuring."

"That's what I'm here for."

# Redneck Riviera

After JD had time to reflect upon the day's events at his "Thinking Spot" under the railroad trestle and hear my "plan" after a quick visit to my house, he went home and matter-of-factly explained his actions on the diamond to Sis and the Rev. Brother-in-Law. He insisted that walking off that field was not only the right thing to do, but also the *Christian* thing to do. They disagreed, but because the Mudcats went on to win the title 12-3 without him, he was begrudgingly forgiven by his parents. I guess Jesus forgave him, too, because he helped the Mudcats win. I'm sure my enjoyment of JD's moment was responsible for a hefty portion of his parents' embarrassment. They strongly suggested he spend less time with me and the new kid from up North. He assured them that not only would he spend less time around me and Jack but also that he had talked things out with Fletch and DC and that they were back to their original plan of sharing the RV in Panama City Beach.

The next morning, I was shoving my kayak into the bed of the Tacoma when JD drove up and hopped out with his duffel bag.

"I see they bought it," I said.

"Hook, line and sinker."

"Religious folks, they're so gullible. I'm proud of you, little sinner."

"Maybe I'll commit a few more this week," he said with a sly grin. "Little ones, of course."

"In that case, you do need to go to church on Sunday," I said with a chuckle. "Gotta cover all your bases, you know."

"Mornin'," Jack said as he shut the door to his apartment. "Where are we going again?"

"The Redneck Riviera," I said as if it were as well known as the French Riviera.

"Panama City Beach," JD clarified. "It's the go-to party spot for spring break and senior trips down here. It's cool that you're going, but you really don't have to feel obligated to go gallivanting with some crazy folks you just met. You could stay and be the interim King of Possum Holler and have this whole place to yourself. Unless you really *want* to go."

"Hey!" I yelled at JD. "There's only *one* King of Possum Holler!"

"Oh, I *want* to go," Jack said as he tossed a satchel into the back seat of the truck cab. "It's one of the items on my summer bucket list anyway. I figured if I'm gonna be this close to Florida, I should see what all the fuss is about. I've never been to any beach south of Atlantic City."

"Damn, that's just sad," I said. "You really do have a lot to learn."

"That's why I'm here," Jack said.

"OK then," JD said. "The more, the merrier. You ready, Uncle Ben?"

"If you don't stop calling me that, I swear—is there anything you need to take besides your bag, like for bodysurfing or killing Jaws?" I asked as I combed through the bed of his pickup truck. "Not that you could find it in all this shit. You're a rolling Tractor Supply, ain't ya? Let's see. Chains, mallets, rope, barbed wire, fencing—you building a prison or something? Did another one of those damn Yankees escape Andersonville? Oh, never mind—there he is," I said while glancing toward Jack with a sly smile.

"I'm a farm boy," JD explained to Jack.

"It's not a farm," I countered for Jack's benefit. "It's a few acres of church property with their house, a chicken coop and a few goats."

"And a donkey," JD argued.

"Oh yeah, and at least one jackass—perhaps a few more."

"You're not gonna be the creepy old uncle preying on young beach girls, are you?" JD asked as we climbed into the truck to begin our unapproved, impromptu, secret getaway.

"Not the only one, no. Look, I'm going to be the drunk tired old creepy uncle chilling out and relaxing while you perverts patrol the beach. Hey, I could use this mallet."

"You could use it when we get back," JD said as he climbed into the front seat of my truck cab. "I've got about 30 feet of fencing to replace."

"Hard pass," I said.

"We sharing a hotel room?" Jack asked, somewhat uncomfortably.

JD shrugged his shoulders to indicate he had no idea. "Knowing Uncle King, he probably booked some cheap motel about four feet off the Strip—Highway 98—with a name like the Dead Squid Inn or the Sea Foam Motel."

"Actually," I said, "I've still got a few tricks up my sleeve."

"Uh-oh," JD said as he turned his head to see Jack buckling his seat belt in the back. "He must've thought the Dead Squid Inn was too fancy. Probably gonna use that mallet to break in somewhere. You may wanna jump out now while you've got a chance."

"I wouldn't if I were you," I said. "In about five hours, you'll thank me. You're about to have a senior trip you'll never forget —if you can remember it."

"Don't worry," Jack said. "Whatever we can't remember, we'll revisit on Instagram."

"Oh, heck no—we gotta keep this on the down-low," JD said. "Remember, I'm not actually with y'all."

"Besides, pictures lie," I explained. "But memories lie even better."

"You should know," JD said. "The older you get, the better you were, right?"

"Actually, the older I get, the *wronger* I was...about everything."

"Can you be *wronger*?" Jack wondered aloud.

"If anybody can be, it's Uncle Ben," JD said.

We shared a laugh and proceeded down the driveway. As I turned south onto Highway 228, I tuned to Radio Margaritaville.

"Oh God!" JD protested. "Jimmy Buffett?"

"You like Buffett!"

"Not for five hours—I'm not a Parrot Head."

"I'm in mourning, dammit!"

"Hasn't it been like nine months?" JD asked.

"So? Jesus died two thousand years ago, and y'all won't shut up about it. Besides, that's not *all* they play. Whatever. What do you want to hear with your good ear?"

"How about some jazz?" Jack suggested. "You know, something chill for the ride."

"I could do some smooth jazz," JD eagerly chimed in. "Not really into any of that so-called *real* jazz that challenges you."

"Oh my God, y'all have the same crappy taste in music. Weirdos."

"Dude, it's your second preset!" JD pointed out.

"Yeah, but I don't *tell* people. Now shut up and chill out! We've got a long way to go and a short time to get there."

"OK, Bandit, but we've literally got *all day* to get there," JD corrected. "Besides, you're unemployed now. You've got time."

"That's the word on the street—well, on the dirt road anyway," I said. "Everybody get on beach time. Don't worry about a thing."

"Thanks, Bob Marley," Jack interjected.

"You're welcome, mon. Actually, that's not a bad idea. Reggae, it is!"

* * *

I hadn't been to Panama City Beach since my senior-year spring break. It was a wild place for teenagers and college students back then, and my conformist ass went along with the beer-drenched flow. I rarely got into trouble around Possum Holler as a kid, and I was lucky I never got arrested down there. I guess there were too many fish in the sea for the cops to catch, and I looked innocent enough. Plenty of others I knew viewed the orange community service vests they earned as a badge of honor or rite of passage. I was quite fine with having dodged that recognition. I don't remember many specifics about those trips other than having a blast. OK, I don't *remember* that, either, but I've been *told* I had a blast. I had a low tolerance for alcohol in my younger days because I didn't get much practice in Possum Holler. I took my studies too seriously. In PC, however, we'd start drinking in the morning and barely slept at night. A friend borrowed his similar-looking older brother's driver's license, and we made a lot of beer runs for folks we met at our motel. We Possum Holler boys made many friends that way.

When JD described those old hotels as having monikers like the "Dead Squid Inn," he wasn't far off. Those old hotels looked as if they were held together with Elmer's Glue, yet they survived tropical storms and hurricanes as well as any steel-and-concrete structures on the coast, maybe better. Wealthier kids stayed at high-rise condos on Thomas Drive, but we poorer kids were rocking the west end of The Strip. I suspect we had more fun and probably got laid more—assuming *twice* that week counted as more. The girls were not picky, and the guys all wore beer goggles. Standards were non-existent, and no one fell in love for more than a day or two.

As my generation became adults, however, we acknowledged the dark side. There were rapes, drug overdoses, alcohol poisonings, and the occasional idiot falling from a balcony. When MTV began airing spring break shows from the beach, it was the beginning of the end of PC's glorious chaos, although folks like me still referred to it as The Redneck Riviera with wistful nostalgia more than condemnation. Ultimately, the Dead Squid Inns of the beach were bought out by more high-rise condominium builders. City leaders decided there was more economic opportunity in attracting families than drunken teenagers. They weren't wrong. After Elizabeth and I had Riley, Panama City Beach was not an option. We took a few cruises and flew to a couple of ultra-safe Caribbean resorts. Our priority was for Riley to have a thrill a minute but stay sheltered from people like—well, a seventeen-year-old version of me. The new Panama City Beach still had pockets of craziness but nothing like my days of drunken cavorting with girls whose names and faces I'd long forgotten. Most of Panama City Beach's beach babes were *actual* babes now, prancing along the surf in ruffled SpongeBob SquarePants bikinis and building sandcastles. The boys on the beach now were reluctant to touch these girls for fear of cooties, pretty mild compared to what some teenagers spread like wildfire three decades earlier. The constants through the wild years and the tame years were the sugar-white sands of the beach and blue-green waters of the Gulf.

JD was more familiar than I was with the new Panama City Beach. Riverside Free Will regularly brought closely monitored youth groups to a Bible retreat called Sands of Grace on the far west end of the Strip. (I referred to it as Grains of Faith because it drew ultra-conservative Christians who were more focused on such issues as who was using which bathroom or whether women were sufficiently subservient.) JD knew every nook and cranny of the retreat as a repeat visitor and as a youth counselor in more recent years. In fact, Riley's March spring break trip from college coincided with JD's latest church excursion to Sands of Grace. They were able to hang out when he got brief breaks from the camp. I had tried in vain to get some inkling from him about how she was really doing, but I also didn't want him to betray Riley's confidence. He was apologetic but insisted that their private conversations had to stay that way, though he said he did vouch for me every now and then. She was no longer speaking to me after what she deemed was the last straw in our relationship—not financially supporting her plan to take the upcoming fall semester off to go backpacking across Europe. I agreed to help out with that dream if she would just wait until after her sophomore year. I wanted to see more serious resolve about her education and future, and I knew she was not mature enough to jet off to Europe on the wings of a poorly researched fool's errand. But her new Daddy Warbucks stepdad pounced on the opportunity to give her—as well as Elizabeth—everything she wanted with no strings attached. I guess Elizabeth's rich husband in New York was everything she had assumed I would be before my brilliant idea of escaping that shallow lifestyle and returning to my roots. After a few months at the old homestead, I vowed I'd never go back to New York or any big city. I thought witnessing my resolution would help Elizabeth and Riley see the light, make the adjustment, and settle into a simpler life. Instead, putting my foot down in that red Georgia clay was the first step toward the end of my dream. They preferred the old shallow me of the city. I may not have known where I fit in Possum Holler as an adult, but I knew I was too far removed to ever fit in again in New York. We couldn't find a middle ground, and Riley disowned me. I doubt I'm the first parent to hear the words "I hate you!" from a teenage girl, but those were the *last* words I heard from her. That no doubt accelerated my recent downward spiral. There was no way I'd drive a wedge between Riley and JD because he was my only window into her world, though that window was a frosted and translucent one at best.

The new me may not have been wealthy enough to satisfy Elizabeth, but I made plenty of money trading online. You've got to have money to make money, and I was one of those lucky bastards who sunk a few hundred dollars into Bitcoin for shits and giggles back when it was a buck. In those early days, a lot of sharp economic minds bought into it as a joke. By the time Bitcoin soared years later, it was such an *old* joke that many of them got hit with a painful punch line—they'd lost the private keys that stood between them and a small or occasionally huge fortune. However, my overly responsible ass did keep a record of my keys and cashed in when the Bitcoin price first crossed $12,000. If I'd had any faith in crypto or just bought a few hundred more early on, I could have been New York rich. Still, my little bit was worth more than $3 million, and that made me Possum Holler rich—especially with an inherited home and land. Despite being Possum Holler rich, though, I rarely splurged. Elizabeth accused me of being cheap, and she managed to convince Riley of the same. Even the Possum Holler folks whom I considered friends decades earlier called me a cheap-ass, though I identify as frugal. Oh, who am I kidding? I *was* cheap, and I didn't have friends anymore. With Riley hating me and my mission of reshaping privileged young minds derailed by the championship incident, I was beginning to feel some of that money burning a hole in the pocket of my cargo shorts (which I scored for just $14 at Wal-Mart, by the way). The urge to finally part with a few bucks led directly to the next two words out of JD's mouth:

"Holy crap!"

"Behold," I said as we looked up toward the sky while I waited to turn into a parking garage. "The Summer Palms Beach Resort. Thirty stories. Three pools. Lazy river. Hot tubs. Basketball court. Beautiful beach. Three nights in the lap of luxury. Beats sharing an RV with a couple of racist pals, huh?"

JD was speechless and nodded with his mouth agape. Jack just smiled. I got the feeling that Jack's family might be more accustomed to this high life than my nephew was.

"If anybody asks, you're brothers and my sons," I said as we made our way to the lobby's front desk. JD had long ago resigned himself to the fact that being around me would always involve some sort of shenanigans. Jack just shrugged his shoulders and grinned. The resort required at least one guest twenty-five or older in each unit, but I had other plans. "Actually, now that I think about it, if anybody asks, tell them to mind their own damn business."

I checked us in and gave each kid a key to room 425.

"Just the fourth floor?" JD asked. "This place is like a hundred stories."

"Thirty," I corrected, "and you're a little picky for a guy with a free vacation, ain't ya? It's not like I planned this trip months ago. Would you like me to call your asshole friends at the RV park and see if they've forgiven you for being a halfway decent human being?"

"Nah, I'm good."

We walked to the elevator and waited. It was time to be a semi-adult for a moment. Even crazy uncles have a few rules.

"Look, I didn't bring y'all down here to go buck wild," I said. "The last thing this beach needs is a whole bunch of 18-year-old Ben Peachys running around here. But whatever's weighing on you—Jack's culture shock and whatever the hell's been gnawing at you, JD—just let it go for a few days. Blow off some steam, and let all that shit back home settle down. I have a feeling you'll see the world a little more clearly from a couple hundred miles away. This is your reset."

"You ain't left Possum Holler in like two years," JD said. "How do you know?"

"Proving my point. My crazy ass needs this, too."

"You *have* been going a little crazy lately."

"*Going*?" I retorted. "Interesting use of present tense."

The elevator door finally opened. They stepped into it, and I pushed my bag toward them but did not board the lift.

"Aren't you coming up?" Jack asked.

"Nope, but take this bag."

"Your clothes are rattling," JD said.

"That's two bottles of tequila, a bottle of triple sec, and two margarita mixers," I explained. "The condo has a blender if you need it. Just don't go crazy. Pace yourself. And don't make a mess or break anything expensive...or anything cheap for that matter. Otherwise, there's just one other rule."

"What's that?" Jack asked.

"I'll be here at 11 a.m. to take y'all to lunch. No pizza or burgers or cheap chain crap from the Strip. We're gonna have one good seafood meal every day, something you can't get at home, really fresh stuff. After that, you're on your own each afternoon and night. And if you meet any trashy girls, your names are Jim Bob and Billy Joe from Phenix City, Alabama."

"And if we meet any *nice* girls?" Jack asked.

"This is Panama City Beach. If you meet any nice girls, they're probably 35 with three kids. But, sure, by all means. Go for it."

"Where are *you* staying?" Jack asked.

"Hooker friend named Sunshine at the end of The Strip. If the trailer's a-rockin', don't come a-knockin'."

JD grabbed the door to keep it from closing, and the two boys looked at each other and rolled their eyes. "Seriously?"

"I am staying at the end of the Strip, the *far* end—at the state park in a tent," I admitted. "This place is too fancy-pants for me, and y'all don't need some old dude weighing you down. Blow off some steam, get it out of your system and then go be responsible human beings for the rest of your lives. This is your free pass. I blew off some steam more than once down here, and even I became a *semi*-responsible human being...until recently anyway. So, anything's possible. See y'all at lunch tomorrow."

* * *

I pitched my two-man pup tent—I assume by "two-man" they meant Kevin Hart and Peter Dinklage—and tied my hammock between a couple of nearby palm trees. I planned to hold a worship service later—just me and the sunset—but that was still hours away, so I lay down in the hammock for a nap to build up the energy for a quick paddle later. The faint sounds of waves rolling ashore on the other side of the park and the warm wind quickly whisked me off to sleep.

I slipped into that all-too-familiar dream in which Riley was in the midst of making a horrible life-changing decision and refusing to listen to me. I don't recall the plot of this one—more just a rapid sequence of images. But the scenes of Riley walking alone into a dark room and then Elizabeth shaking her head at me in disapproval were still fresh and haunted me when I was awakened by a redneck's pickup truck revving its engine to fire up its enhanced exhaust pipes. Folks who drive vehicles that are altered to be noisier or who blast their radios strike me as desperate for attention. I think each one should have a bumper sticker that reads: "Please notice me—my mommy didn't show me enough love as a child." Of course, thirty-seven years earlier, I was hanging out with just those types of loud folks on The Strip—guys hollering out windows while stuck in traffic jams, girls squealing and flashing their boobs, and, of course, those damn thumping car radios. That *was* paradise. Now, it sounds like a nightmare, and I didn't want any part of it. All I wanted was a little peace, which had been hard to find lately, even on the twenty-two acres of my Possum Holler kingdom.

"Sorry pieces of shit," I grumbled as I rolled out of the hammock with all the grace my weary ass could muster—meaning my rollout left me stomach-down on the sandy ground. Then I looked at my watch. "Damn."

It was six-thirty. I'd snoozed far longer than expected, and it was too late to drag my kayak to a launching spot. I took ten deep breaths to relax myself and tried to tune out the fading truck engine. My simple goal was to relax—something I never attempted as a kid on The Redneck Riviera. I'd left all the alcohol with the boys because I wanted to be sober for a change. Well, mostly sober. I chewed a couple of perfectly legal but very potent Delta-9 gummies, grabbed a beach towel and headed down a well-trodden path to the park's quiet beach for my rendezvous with the sunset—*my* church. I knew somewhere between the gummies and the sun was likely where I'd find any sliver of nirvana. It was as close to meditating as I could get. Don't get me wrong—I totally get the point of meditating and could have used the spiritual reset, but I didn't think meditating while repeating my then-mantra of "om-fuck-my-life" would be all that helpful.

It had been a month since I'd last consumed a gummy—something I realized when they kicked in twenty minutes earlier than usual. I clearly had grown less tolerant during that month, or perhaps it was pure coincidence that my legs felt like they weighed three tons each. *They* were meditating quite well, totally zoned out, and they weren't going *anywhere*. As usual, though, the gummies fired up my synapses and sharpened every sight and sound. The swooping seagulls sounded like attacking spaceships, and the sun was the largest it had ever been, taking over half the sky. The waves looked somewhere between four and forty feet high. I turned my heavy skull to glance at my watch. It was 7:30.

But which *day*?

Oh shit, I thought, I spent all night out here; it's *tomorrow* night! The warm, salty air massaged my face while the gently rolling waves lulled me deeper into my trance. For the first time in my life, I was having a religious experience. I'd been on the beach for just an hour, and it was already the second sunset I'd witnessed.

After what felt like three more nights on the beach—or two hours if you believe in watches and time—I began the trek back to the primitive campground where I'd pitched the tent. I zig-zagged in the moonlight as my legs lightened up to only a few hundred pounds each. Just keep heading east, I told myself. I couldn't find the primitive campground but soon found myself in a sea of RVs. Several had lights strung along their awnings, and laughter rang out from a few along with the kind of modern mud-god-gun-flag country music that always made my head ache.

"You all right, buddy?" an older gentleman with a Santa-style beard asked from his outdoor rocking chair as some whiny country singer rambled on about how small town he was even though he was probably from Chicago or LA. I wanted to sit for a moment but not at the risk of getting that horrid song and the next twenty just like it stuck in my head.

"Nah, I'm great. Thanks, though."

As I neared the end of a long row of campers, I decided they must have mowed down the primitive campground during the week or so that I'd been sitting on the beach. Damn, I thought—I've gone from a king to *homeless*.

Then I heard the call of *my* wild side—the pinging of steel drums, whir of a blender, and the voice of the messiah of margaritas. I couldn't imagine where my tent was, but these were the kind of folks I could hang with, even if they were imaginary.

"Phinz up!" I mumbled as I approached the Parrot Head setup. My imagination wasn't creative enough to make such a setup this realistic.

"Hey there," a bleach-blonde lady in a Hawaiian shirt responded. "Buffett fan, huh?"

"Does a bear shit in the woods?" I responded.

"I assume so, and I'm gonna take that as a yes," she said with a laugh. "Have a seat. Join our mini-tailgate."

I tried to shake myself alert and not appear high. I knew the gummies had less effect when I was moving, but I was tired of walking. This lady appeared about my age and seemed harmless enough. She was a Parrot Head, after all. We're good people. I'd been around thousands of Parrot Heads tailgating before Buffett shows for more than twenty-five years, and the biggest issues were trying to keep people from being too friendly or too generous as everyone wearing a lei, hula skirt, or coconut shell bra tried to force another free drink or leftover cheeseburgers down your throat. The only fights that broke out were between Tums and heartburn. Unfortunately, I hadn't been to one of those concerts in more than a decade, when I was still mildly social. The days of wanting to be shoulder-to-shoulder with thousands of people—even *my* people—had passed. And with the old man gone, there would never be another experience that compared. That sailboat had left port.

I could handle a *handful* of like-minded souls for a little while, though, especially since I was haunted by the regret of passing on a few opportunities to revisit the tequila-soaked promised land of a Buffett show in the previous ten years. Like-minded souls were hard to find back in Possum Holler. Even the Parrot Heads I'd met through the years at concerts were like-minded only during the moments we were wastin' away together. After the tailgates and shows, everybody went back to their regularly scheduled programming. Many of them were very un-Parrot-Head-y in their day-to-day conformist lives.

"Well, thanks. What's the tailgate for?" I asked as I plopped down in a standard outdoor bag chair, the kind you might find on sale at the entrance of a Buc-ee's along the interstate.

"Concert replay. You want a drink?"

"What you got?"

"You're joking, right?" she said with a laugh. "Hey, Jenny! Bring an extra one. I found another Parrot Head creeping around."

"A step ahead of you," said the woman emerging from the RV with a red solo cup in each hand. My brain tingled from turning my heavy skull too quickly to see her. She was fit, as if she had once been an athlete, her light brown hair with faint gray streaks tied into a ponytail. She didn't seem to be the type to spend a lot of time on makeup, hair, or plumping up her lips and other parts. She had a natural, carefree attractiveness. Then again, she wouldn't be the first middle-aged lady to forego that kind of stuff at the beach for a few days.

"Hi, I'm Jenny," she said as she handed me a drink and then sat on a large red plastic cooler.

"Ben," I said.

"You look strangely familiar," she said as she pushed a couple of stray bangs out of her eyes.

"I think you mean I look strange," I said. "I'm not from around here. In fact, I haven't even been to Florida in years."

"You're not from Thomasville, Georgia, are you?"

"No, a couple hours north of there, in fact. Andersonville. You know, where the infamous Civil War prison was? I used to work there."

"In the museum or with the park service?" she asked.

"No, during the war," I said. The gummies may have diminished my coordination and judgment, but my smart-ass attitude was impervious.

"No family in Thomasville? You must have a doppelganger there then because I swear I *know* that face."

"I don't know you well enough to discuss my doppelganger in public, but I did know a girl from Thomasville *waaay* back when," I said. "First girl I ever kissed—during tennis camp at Florida State. Poor girl. I had no clue what I was doing."

"Ahh," she said as she looked downward for a second and then scratched her temple. "Your first kiss wouldn't happen to have been some super cute and extremely talented tennis player named Jennifer Jacobs, would it?"

"Well, yes, but how'd you—wait, what?"

"Jenny Jacobs at your service, Ben Peachy. Well, Jenny Thompson now."

"Holy shit!" I stammered. My gummies had really upped their game with this mind trick. This was way too random to be real, but I didn't see any point in screwing up the hallucination. It had real life beat by a mile. "How the hell did you remember my name?"

"Well, I can count the number of people I've met named Peachy on one hand—one *finger* actually. I thought about looking you up after that camp, but then I remembered that kiss and figured, why bother?"

Jennifer Jacobs was indeed my first kiss. We met at summer tennis camp after my freshman year of high school. Florida State University had multiple sports camps going on at once, but most of the attendees were baseball players as FSU was a perennial College World Series contender. The much smaller tennis portion of the camp was co-ed, and they put the boys and girls tennis players together in the same hall on the bottom floor of Cash Hall. Fortunately for us, we were chaperoned by two players from the FSU team who let us run wild after our morning and afternoon sessions were over. I was uncool even by freshman standards, and this Jennifer Jacobs a few rooms down was out of my league—not to mention she was an experienced older woman, a *sophomore*. The camp leader paired us up for an intracamp mixed doubles tournament, and she took a liking to—or perhaps pity upon—me. Maybe she didn't have extra time to hunt for a more desirable guy. We found ourselves awake at midnight the day before camp was to end, a few hours after we finished second in the tournament. She'd given me about twenty openings to go in for a kiss, but I was too nervous to make the first move. Fortunately, she finally gave me a subtle nudge.

"You gonna kiss me or what?" she finally asked. "It's getting late."

Gulp. I figured it might be my last-ever chance to figure out what a French kiss was. I went in mouth open and tongue flying around like an Irish setter hanging out of a car window. I was too self-conscious to enjoy it. Was my tongue going the right way? Should I try counter-clockwise? Was there too much spit in my mouth? Was she thinking that it was a lot like kissing an Irish setter? Based upon the recollection she had just shared, the latter must have been true. Fortunately, we spent the next two hours that night twirling tongues until I fell in love. We slept in the same bed that night, but I'd barely learned how to French kiss, so I damn sure didn't attempt any further experiments. I didn't know much about the opposite sex back then, but, by golly, I knew when to leave well enough alone.

Our torrid love affair was over by the next morning. I asked for her phone number, but she refused, saying she had a boyfriend. I'd gained and lost the love of my life in less than twenty-four hours, but at least I'd finally got me one of those French kisses everybody had been talking about, and I was eager to try some of that tongue-twisting with new victims back home.

"Oh, come on," I argued with a smile as I arrived back on Earth. "My kisses couldn't have been *that* bad."

"Allison," she said as she turned to her friend, "have you ever kissed your dog in the mouth?" she asked with a laugh.

Whoa, way too coincidental, I thought.

"Hey, I got better...over time, I think," I rebutted.

"That's because you had a good teacher," she replied with a wink.

"Can't argue with that. You broke my heart, by the way."

"What? It was *one* night!"

"The greatest two hours of my fourteen-year-old life! And then you had to go back to some stupid boyfriend!"

"If it makes you feel any better, he became my stupid husband."

"*Ex*-stupid husband," Allison chimed in.

"As an *ex*-stupid husband myself, I think I'm offended."

"Then you need to toughen up, buttercup," Jenny said as she placed her hand on my shoulder. "I'm afraid I've gotten to the age where the filter between my brain and mouth doesn't work."

"Well, I'm a very sensitive person, a gentle soul who simply wants to get along with everyone."

"I'm calling bullshit," she said with a chuckle.

"What's his number?"

"Huh?"

"Sorry, I assumed that was your ex-husband's name," I said.

We talked for an hour and had another margarita as the Buffett concert continued to replay in the background. As Jimmy finished his first encore from the quarter-century-old show, Allison excused herself and stepped into the camper. Buffett's second encore in the old days was usually one slow song with just Jimmy and his guitar, something to settle folks down before they exited the arena and embarked upon trying to locate their vehicles in the lots where they'd spent the afternoon tailgating. We heard the crowd cheer as he came back out and began playing the ballad "Changing Channels."

"Ooo, I love this song!" she said as she grabbed my hand and pulled. "Dance with me."

"OK, but go slow. I think those margaritas are mixing with my gummies."

"Wow, you *are* a wild man now."

"Is *wild* a synonym for tired and too old to behave like a 14-year-old?" I asked facetiously as we began to sway back and forth with her hands cupped behind my neck. She kept pulling herself closer as I concentrated on not falling down. The Earth's speed had picked up pace, going too fast even for my dorky two-step. As the song faded, she went in for a kiss. I was relieved that it was a light peck upon my lips—I was too wobbly for any tongue twisting. I didn't want her to think I hadn't improved in that department and that kissing me was now more like kissing an aging Saint Bernard.

"What the fuck?!" a deep male voice blared.

Jenny pushed back, her mouth agape.

"What are you doing here, Billy?!"

Billy was a tall yet round fellow with a beer gut that couldn't be wholly contained by his white t-shirt. He sported a red trucker cap, dirty blue jeans, and boots. He was a walking stereotype, and he added up to about two of me.

"Let me guess," I whispered to Jenny, "the stupid ex? Mr. Bullshit?"

"Well," she whispered, "*almost* ex."

"Denny said he saw y'all at Ms. Newby's and that y'all were down here in *my* camper!" he yelled.

"*Our* camper," she corrected. "I told you Allison and I were going to use it. You're not supposed to be within 100 yards."

"So you can run around with motherfuckers like this?"

"Look," I said as I turned to reason with the man, "I—"

He slugged me in the jaw, knocking my already unsteady ass to the ground while he lost his balance and tripped over the girls' cooler, making him angrier. Allison came running out of the camper and began screaming that she was going to call the cops. Billy scrambled back to his feet while I sat there and shook the cobwebs out of my gummified head.

"Stop it, Billy!" Jenny screamed. "He's drunk!"

"So am I!"

"Then you need to get the hell out of here before the cops come!" Allison yelled.

"I ain't going nowhere," he said.

"Actually, that's a double-negative," I said, still sitting in the dirt and rubbing my head. "If you're not going nowhere, then you *are* going somewhere. It's pretty basic English."

"Who the hell is this smart-ass?" Billy asked.

"Maybe you better leave," Jenny quietly suggested to me as she helped me stand.

"Yeah, maybe I better leave," I parroted. "I recently lost my dental insurance. Not that this wasn't fun. You going to be OK? Seriously."

"He won't do anything with Allison here," she insisted. "We'll be all right. We know how to calm him down. The tent area you're looking for is a couple hundred yards that way, around the curve. I'm sorry you got caught up in my bullshit on what was shaping up to be a pretty fun night, huh?"

"Yeah, thank goodness I don't have any personal drama myself, at least none that's *physically* painful," I said with a smile. I gave an embarrassed goodbye wave to Allison and began walking in the direction she had pointed when I felt the heel of Billy's boot in my lower back, sending me stumbling forward until I lost my balance again and landed facedown in the dirt and gravel. As Billy laughed, I stood back up and faced the three. I was tired and exasperated. How the hell could she have broken my fourteen-year-old heart for this redneck asshole? I mean, geez, every sad song that came on the rest of that summer reminded me of our two-hour love affair. I still get misty-eyed when I hear Madonna's "Crazy for You." Unfortunately, in my inebriated state, all I could muster out of my mouth was, "Really?" Billy grinned as Jenny looked down and Allison stepped in front of the large redneck. I stumbled the next couple of hundred yards back toward the primitive campground as the arguing grew more faint behind me.

"Whew," I said aloud as I spotted my truck and the pup tent beside it. "Home sweet home." I crawled in, zipped the opening and listened for any boot stomps coming to finish me off. Within moments, I was out—or as good ol' Billy likely would put it, O-W-T, *owt.*

# The Best Times You'll Never Remember

There's nothing quite like waking up near a Florida beach, where squawking seagulls remind you that each new day is a clean slate and that every last night could be a huge mistake somebody else remembers more vividly than you.

There were a couple of nights during my senior year when I woke up in a cheap Panama City Beach motel next to a beautiful girl while having no idea who she was nor what we'd done—only that whatever occurred involved misplacing my underwear. I'd rub my head, smile, and think, "Looks like I had fun." Then they'd wake and look around the room bewilderedly with a fake smile that spoke volumes, such as, "Looks like you had fun, and I hope you don't have a raging case of crabs."

On this particular morning, I once again was missing underwear but only because I rarely wore them after turning fifty unless I had to stand in front of a class of teenagers. It's not like I was hitting the gym or tennis courts and needed to keep the twig and berries restrained. I'd rather my body be comfortable while my well-intentioned missteps piled up and crushed my spirit. Unlike those high school days, however, I woke up with no fear that I'd picked up an STD from a stranger. Then it hit me.

"Jenny," I whispered aloud. I rubbed my head and tried to recall the hallucinations of the previous night. I knew they were vivid at the time, but they had become mighty foggy in the morning light. I wished I hadn't conjured up that giant redneck because I had one hell of an imaginary headache. Two gummies were one too many. I was still new to the stuff and had yet to find the happy zone between a light buzz and whacked out.

I unzipped the tent and went outside for a stretch and a whiz before the rest of the park woke up to reflect upon *their* mistakes from the prior evening. I zipped my shorts just before a truck pulling a small camper passed me on its way along the gravel road to the RV section of the park. I threw on a Braves baseball cap and flip-flops and wandered up the gravel road behind the camper.

"Anything's possible," I mumbled aloud. Talking to myself was becoming more of a thing each day as I further descended into a comfortable loneliness. The only hope I had left in the world was that Riley's current rebellion was a phase and that she'd someday recall that she was once daddy's little angel—and happy. But that was years ago. As for other girls, the older ones, I'd given up hope of being happy with any woman, be it my remarried Elizabeth, Jennifer Jacobs from tennis camp, or Jenny Thompson of the previous night's imaginary Buffett concert and bubba beatdown. I hadn't sworn off women, mind you—I just wasn't interested in extremes, be they joy or drama, and I feared that any new relationship had the potential to bring both at the same time. I couldn't handle anyone else's emotional fringes while I waited for my life to settle down, not that I was taking any positive steps away from my own cliffs.

As I entered the RV section, I noticed that the first slot was empty. It was unusual for *any* RV slot in all of Panama City Beach to be empty during summer months. I flashed back through the mental scrapbook of my gummy trip and recalled the ladies' RV with its blue awning, sling chairs, and plastic palm tree aglow. Wasn't it in this first slot? It seemed unlikely they could have packed up and left so quickly, confirming that it must have been my mind playing tricks on me after all. It's a damn shame, for imaginary Jenny had aged quite well—far better than I had.

"Oh, crap!" I said as I glanced at my fraying sports watch that I never took off, even to shower, because it was too much work to put it back on. "It's lunchtime."

I raced back to the tent, threw on a UGA baseball cap and t-shirt, sprayed on a little stink-good (as my grandmother called it), and headed to get the boys for a good lunch.

* * *

It was 11:30 Central time as the elevator began its ascent to the fourth floor of Summer Palms. I feared what I might find when the boys opened the door. Leaving them with two bottles of tequila might not have been my smartest move, though it had plenty of competition for dumbest recent move. I didn't want to spend my life savings on a trashed condo.

"Holy hell!" JD said as he swung open the door after a couple of knocks.

"Ain't that an oxymoron?" I asked as I walked in. "Geez, I'm just 45 minutes late."

"What the hell happened to you?" Jack asked as he came into the main room from the balcony, sliding the glass door shut behind him.

"What are you talking about?"

"Your face," JD said.

"I was born with it. You should be used to it by now."

"No, it's even worse than usual. You clearly haven't seen a mirror," JD said as he motioned toward a full-length mirror in the hallway.

"Damn," I said aloud as I saw a severely blackened left eye and a large raspberry on my right cheek.

"What happened?" JD asked.

"Well, it's kind of hard to explain, but I think it was a bad dream."

"You got beat up in a dream?" Jack followed up. "There wasn't a guy in a striped shirt named Freddy in this dream, was there? All burned up? Hat? Blades for fingers?"

"I didn't say it made sense."

"Well, we're starving, but we can't go to a decent restaurant with you looking like you got run over by a garbage truck," JD said. "So where are we going?"

"It was going to be The Captain's Table, a joint in town where the locals go, but, yeah, we probably should go someplace where I'd fit in a little better."

"The county jail?" JD suggested.

"Actually, I passed some generic Waffle Huddle Pancake Omelet Coffee Kettle Shack House on the way," I said. "Probably fit right in. Hey, wait a minute? What did *y'all* do last night?"

I asked because their condo was freakishly tidy. Their beds were even made. The kitchen counters were clear with the exception of the two bottles of tequila—two still slam-full bottles of tequila.

"Played chess," Jack said.

"And someone left a bottle of wine in the fridge," JD added. "We hit that."

"Y'all can play chess at home," I argued. "I brought y'all down here to blow off some steam, indulge in some questionable behavior, find that balance."

"Maybe we don't have as much crazy to get out of our system as you do," JD said. "We got some beach time in, though. But I'll tell you what: Today, I promise we'll make a frozen margarita in honor of you."

"*A* margarita? One? This is Panama City Beach. The Redneck Riviera! Y'all gotta loosen up!"

"Yeah, if we put a little effort into it, maybe we can get our asses whupped, too," Jack chimed in. He seemed a little too excited to get into the ribbing—more like an extended family member than a random renter doing summer research.

"That's more like it," I said. "Now let's go get waffles and something—God-willing—scattered and smothered and diced and chunked."

"Like your face," JD said with a laugh.

"Smart ass."

"Cut me some slack," he retorted. "It's hard raising an uncle."

* * *

There was one booth available at the generic breakfast joint. I sat on one side and slid over to make room for JD, but he and Jack seated themselves together opposite me. They were acting as if they had known each other for years instead of days. Then again, they were the two skinnier ones. It was a better fit.

"Smells delicious," Jack said.

"It's called grease," I explained, "the primary ingredient in all that is holy. They probably don't have it in Boston. It's the actual reason I moved back South."

Jack scanned the clientele, half of whom looked like Kid Rock after a post-show bender—and those were the ladies. He then glanced at the griddle where hashbrowns, bacon, and sausage were sizzling as the cook looked downward, not acknowledging the constant barking of orders from haggard waitresses rotating between customers, coffee pots, and smoke breaks. They appeared to be about eighty-five years old but probably were closer to forty.

"Are you sure it's a good idea to eat here?" Jack asked.

"Of course," I said. "It's always a good idea to eat at a joint like this...at first."

"And afterward?"

"Then you find out why it's a stupid idea," JD said.

"Duh," I confirmed. "That's when it becomes full-circle, like a pancake. Mmm, pancakes."

"We don't have pancakes, just waffles," corrected a waitress who bore a striking resemblance to Willie Nelson.

"Nah, I can't do squares today," I said while shaking my head as if my life had been ruined by the pancake news. I ordered a ham-and-cheese omelet with covered hash browns, though I was most interested in the coffee. JD ordered a huge special of waffles, eggs, bacon and grits with a sweet tea. Jack embarrassed me by ordering a salad.

"Jesus," I said. "I didn't even know they *had* salads here."

"You can change your order and get one," JD said.

"No, no. I'm a guy. So, what did y'all do last night besides sip wine and play chess? Discuss romance novels? Needlepoint?"

They told me they spent the afternoon bodysurfing in the Gulf with some cheap boards they got from a beach shop across The Strip. They wore themselves out on the waves until the sun began to set, and then they donated their boards to a family with a couple of young boys. They then had a pizza delivered and began their wild night of wine and chess. Afterward, they sat on the balcony and talked...for hours.

"Talked?"

"Yeah," JD said. "It's like when your mouth moves up and down and words come out in the direction of another human being."

"Eww. Weirdos."

I was lonely after Elizabeth and then Riley left me alone in Possum Holler, but the last thing I wanted to do was *talk* about it, especially with another *guy*. Why would I share feelings when I could privately wallow in them? No, rather than talk, I was more apt to drown my feelings in liquor, and, all too recently, gummies. JD, meanwhile, always had moved effortlessly between high school cliques and counted jocks, nerds, druggies, churchy folks and everyone in between as friends. He knew how to talk to anyone. He enjoyed Sunday school and hymns on Sunday mornings and then watching a Braves game and nursing a beer at my house on Sunday afternoons. Though he got along with everyone back home, the ease with which he and Jack connected unsettled me. While they came from two totally different worlds, they seemed to have many common interests right off the bat. I doubted my sister Sarah would be comfortable even with the concept of a chess buddy, much less the fleeting possibility that quickly breezed through my brain. "Nah," I thought. "No way."

"So, seriously," Jack asked, "what happened to you last night? Kinda worried."

"Apparently, I was a little inebriated and fell down—a lot, it seems."

The boys looked at each other to see if either was buying my story. Neither was, but even I wasn't sure if the truth was true. My authentic memory seemed way more far-fetched.

"You said we need to find some balance, blow off a little steam," JD said.

"And?"

"Maybe you need to find a little balance yourself," JD said in all seriousness. "Whatever happened last night, it can't be good. I know some things have gone off the rails for you in the last few years, and God knows I miss Riley, too. But you're family, Uncle Ben. You used to be easy going and had that light in your eye. You don't have to care what happens to you, but I do. And I know Riley does, too."

"Fine," I said. "I'll do what I originally intended tonight—walk the beach, kayak, watch the sunset, read a book. Y'all should be the ones blowing off steam. I'll be a mature human being for a change."

"Hopefully, we can do that in a less painful way," Jack asked.

"Yeah, it's probably best if I bring y'all back in one piece," I said, nodding toward JD, "especially since your folks think you're down here with your friends."

"I am," JD said as he tapped his glass of sweet tea with Jack's glass of unsweetened tea. "New friends anyway."

"Y'all are so weird."

* * *

I held up my end of the bargain that afternoon. I earnestly hoped the beach could refresh my soul or at least infuse me with enough hope, false or not, to keep going until Riley came to her senses and realized I wasn't Beelzebubba. I was jobless but comfortable enough financially to ride out the rest of my simple life in Possum Holler if I so chose. Work was optional, and I was content to opt out for a bit. What I needed was purpose. I doubted the meaning of my life would wash up on the shores of St. Andrews State Park, but there was no harm in giving it a shot. So, that afternoon, I bopped around the shallows of the Intracoastal in my kayak and met a couple of dolphins. If I'd have taken a gummy beforehand, we might have had a chat, but I was determined to play it straight. Sure enough, they were ordinary, non-talking dolphins—my kind of mammals. Later, I stretched out a towel upon the beach and sat down with a small cooler. I took a sip of the first diet root beer, my go-to non-alcoholic drink.

"Ahh," I whispered to myself. "Yep, gettin' wild tonight."

I didn't know how right I was until my phone buzzed. It was Jack.

"What's up?" I answered.

"We took your advice to heart, perhaps a little too much."

"How so?"

"We made a pitcher of margaritas, and then JD got a call. I think it was a girl. He just clammed up for a minute or two and had this blank look on his face. I asked if he wanted to talk about it, and then he said he wanted to get shit-faced."

"That definitely doesn't sound like JD," I said. "I've never even seen him catch a buzz."

"Well, after a couple more pitchers, he was plastered. Now I can't find him. He went out to get some air and disappeared. I'm worried. I didn't like the look on his face."

"I'm on the way."

* * *

I met Jack in the lobby and dispatched him to walk west along the beach. I headed east. I figured if JD truly were drunk, he wouldn't stray too far in the Florida heat, so we agreed to meet back up in a half-hour at the hotel pool. I was relieved to see the boys together by the pool as I returned from my search. They were talking with a group of guys above them on a third-floor balcony. As I got closer, though, I realized this was no polite chat. Then I heard one of the third-floor boys yell the words "Fucking faggot!" JD jumped, grabbed hold of the second-floor balcony railing, and began scaling the exterior toward the boys like an enraged extra in *Planet of the Apes*.

"What the—" I said as I began running. "JD!"

He was outnumbered, and he was indeed going to get his ass whupped—and not by potentially imaginary foes as I did. He was a strapping young man, but he was no experienced fighter. Before the third-floor boys could get their hands on him, though, JD slipped. His arms flailed but couldn't find anything solid to grab during the one-second fall that seemed more like a minute to me. His legs banged on a chaise lounge and his head smacked the concrete. I grabbed him and placed my hand over a bleeding spot in the back of his skull as Jack frantically called 9-1-1. JD was out cold.

A hotel employee rushed to the scene and just muttered, "Every damn summer."

I glared at him, then turned my eyes toward the third floor. The loudmouths were gone, likely fleeing the scene before any cops came.

It was less than three minutes before paramedics were jogging toward us. This was an emergency to us, but it seemed like they just saw it as a typical Wednesday. They likely spent many days going up and down The Strip waiting for calls to help teenagers who'd fallen, drank too much, or overdosed. They pushed us aside and got JD sitting upright. His eyes opened, but he looked confused. He winced and reached for his left leg, which had absorbed much of the blow against the metal arm of the chaise. In another couple of minutes, he was on his way to the hospital across the bay in Panama City. Jack and I hopped in the truck and tailed them.

An hour later, a doctor approached us in the ER waiting area and reported that JD had a concussion but was otherwise just badly bruised. I asked if there was any chance of amnesia or memory loss, and he said if we were in a movie, almost definitely, but unlikely in the real world—though not unheard of. He also noted that JD was quite intoxicated—a point he made while staring directly at me—and said that any memory loss was more likely from being drunk than from a bump on the head. He clearly was annoyed and told us while briskly walking away that he was keeping JD overnight for observation and family members could visit him in about an hour. Jack and I glanced at each other. Family members? Damn, I hadn't thought about having to call my sister. I dreaded that phone conversation, one that could wait at least an hour until we had a chance to see JD in his hospital bed and verify that he was OK for ourselves. Afterward, I would have to bite the bullet.

"What?!" was how she answered. At least I knew she still had my contact information on her phone.

"Hey, Sis. Um, JD is fine, but he bumped his head pretty good and is going to spend the night in the hospital," I said.

"I'm sorry—what?! He's in Panama City! Where are *you*?"

"Panama City."

"What?!"

"He's fine, Sis. He didn't feel comfortable with his racist friends, so I offered to put him and Jack up at a nice condo down here so he could enjoy his senior trip. He deserves it."

"Who is *Jack*? Is that the weird kid with you at the baseball game?"

"I'm renting out Riley's apartment, and he's the first person to stay there. He's a sharp college kid doing some research, and he and JD just hit it off. Turns out they're kindred spirits."

"The only spirits you know about are at the liquor store! Is he in the main hospital? What room?"

"306, but he's sleeping. Doctor says he should be fine and can leave in the morning."

"I'm on the way! Pack his stuff! I'm bringing him home and away from your evil influence, you spawn of Satan!"

"C'mon, Sis, you—wait, our Dad was the dark prince?"

"Pack it!"

If she had an old school landline, my eardrum might have been busted by her slamming the phone. Instead, I suspect she damn near broke her finger furiously pressing the "end" button.

* * *

JD was fast asleep, so Jack and I headed to the condo to pack his stuff. I knew I'd overstepped my boundaries with JD. If I'd simply paid for a hotel room and left the boys to it, this incident may never have happened. Yet, I'd supplied them with alcohol and encouraged them to explore their wild sides, or at least find out if they had one. I had no idea JD would take it to heart. He'd always been a model of moderation—fun enough to be one of the guys at school with just enough Christian guilt in his veins to keep him from committing unforgivable sins. He found a balance few kids his age had achieved or sought. This was way out of character. This was the second major snap in a single week. I was proud of the first one, but the second filled me with shame.

"You say some girl called?" I asked Jack as we reached the top of the Hathaway Bridge that connected Panama City proper with Panama City Beach. "You know who?"

"No," Jack said simply. "I gave him some privacy. He didn't say anything after, just, 'I need a drink.' He wouldn't tell me anything else. I didn't pry."

"Weird," I said. "I mean, he's been out with plenty of girls, but never anything serious—dates at dances and parties and stuff like that. I hope nothing happened back home. It seems like some kid gets hurt in a car wreck every year about the time school gets out."

"I don't know," he said as he stared out the window at the dark bay. "We talked a lot the night before, but he definitely keeps a few things to himself. And I don't know him well enough to push. I mean, we barely know each other, right?"

"Something's been eating at him," I said. "Maybe he's just drifting a little bit. I know the feeling. But he'll get his shit straight. Just gotta get over this hump, whatever it is."

Per my sister's demands, we packed JD's duffel bag with his clothes, phone charger and toiletries. If anything was left behind, we could bring it home in a couple of days. I had the condo rented for two more nights, so I decided to take over JD's room and abandon the state park. I told Jack he could do whatever he wanted to, but that I'd be happy to help him experience the real Gulf beyond the craziness of the Redneck Riviera's Strip. He'd seen enough of the wild side to scare him. But there's more to the Gulf Coast than condos, liquor stores, souvenir shops, and overpriced, overrated restaurants. You just have to get your feet wet to truly appreciate the real Gulf behind the wild wizard's curtain.

After packing, we returned to the hospital to face the music. Sarah was just two years older than I, but we'd never been close. While I had my share of teenage moments that I was thankful my parents never found out about, I was still considered a goody-two-shoes in our little neck of the woods. I got excellent grades, participated in a few school clubs, and, as I mentioned, played high school tennis for nearby Macon County High School. Though our home was technically inside the Sumter County line, Americus High and Sumter County High were too far away, and my folks were afraid that Muckalee Christian might steer us, ironically, toward *less* Christian behavior. My dad referred to the Muckalee folks as *ChrINOs*—Christians In Name Only. So, Sarah and I attended Macon County public schools by using our great aunt's home address. The school was closer to our home, and we could literally walk to our great aunt's house in a matter of minutes down a red dirt road, so it wasn't the biggest school zoning crime in history. It wasn't like we were faking our residency so I could start at quarterback for some prep powerhouse. I could barely throw a spiral. Besides, the Macon County school system likely would have looked the other way about my residency had they known because I didn't exactly drag down the collective GPA. In fact, I was the first to ace the math portion of the SAT—or so I was told by our guidance counselor.

Sarah was a different story. *She* was the bad apple back then. I had plenty of doubts about religion in my childhood, but I went to church every week with my parents, who, thankfully, allowed me to question dogma and ponder spiritual matters for myself. My father never pushed me to get baptized and told me that it was something I needed to feel and decide for myself. I never felt the call and never got baptized, and I drifted from the church completely after leaving Possum Holler for Brown. Sarah, meanwhile, believed all the religious stuff and was baptized when she was eleven years old, but she felt too full of sin to show her face in church as a teenager. She was a pot-smoking wild girl who tried to walk a fine line between fun girl and whore, though she often tripped over it. She'd have never made it at Muckalee Christian, but she had plenty of friends at Macon County High, many of them druggies and potheads—or as they were known at my school in the early nineties, the cool kids. I was neither cool nor ostracized. I could get along with most any clique, much like JD, but, unlike JD, I wasn't embraced by any of them. I was just kind of *there* on the fringes. I was wallpaper—which, quite frankly, the school could have used on the off-white cinderblock halls that were nearly as bland as I was.

Sarah barely graduated high school, and college was not a viable option for her. As soon as she got her diploma, she took off with a boyfriend to New York City, where he was determined to become the next great punk guitarist—more than ten years after punk had pretty much died. I'm not sure how much my parents heard from Sarah, but she and I didn't see each other or speak for years. She was never home when I went back to Possum Holler for Christmas. Somewhere along the way, though, Sarah saw the light—or was blinded by it. She lost her wannabe Ramone, went through a few more, found Jesus, married the preacher man, and became a mother. As soon as she had the baby, Sarah and the preacher man moved back to Possum Holler and became the model church family. She believed her sins had been washed away, and I replaced her as the family heathen, though I never officially received the memo about the promotion. I didn't like being around my sinful sister when I was young, but I truly loathed being around my churchy, saved sister even more.

When Jack and I arrived at JD's room to warn him the parents were on the way, he was groggy and didn't remember the fall nor what led up to it. We filled him as best we could so that he could brace himself for the parental interrogation. An hour later, the door swung open. It was dear sister Sarah and the Rev. Ronnie. She glared at me but said nothing as she marched past. The lasers shooting from her eyes through my skull spoke loudly enough.

"He's fine," I told Ronnie as Sarah began caressing JD's head.

Ronnie's furry eyebrows rose, crinkling the pale forehead of his massive bald cranium. "We need to talk," he said matter-of-factly.

I sent Jack to wait in the downstairs lobby so that I could be privately admonished in the hallway. I had it coming. Even by crazy uncle standards, I'd crossed a line.

"I know what you're going to say," I began.

"I don't think you do," he retorted. "I know JD's gonna be fine. We prayed about it the whole way down. And, we prayed for you, too."

"To be hit by a train?"

"That did cross my mind, but it looks like that's already happened," Ronnie said with a half-smile. "We're worried about you, Ben. You've been spiraling out of control, and it's understandable. I know losing Riley hurts. But we don't need JD spiraling, too. Like it or not, you and Sarah are family. JD's caught in the middle of you two, and that probably has a lot to do with why he's been kind of *off* lately."

"Sarah and I are very, *very* different people, Ronnie."

"I know you're hurting, and I wish you had something in here," he added as he touched my chest, "to help you fill that void—besides liquor and encouraging disruptive behavior."

"I'm not going to church, Ronnie, if that's what you're getting at. And JD's too sharp for Sarah and I to convince him we've made peace. And, just so you'll know, I had nothing to do with what JD did that day on that baseball field. I am proud of him for standing up for that kid, but I was as surprised as everybody else. And I'm still not sure what led up to him bumping his head."

"He's been quieter lately. He used to participate in Sunday school, ask thoughtful questions. His friends mattered to him more than they do now. Baseball and competing for a state title meant *everything* just a few weeks ago. He was going to walk on at Georgia Southwestern, but I'm afraid that may not be an option now. He needs something to anchor him, a focus. He needs spiritual renewal. He needs positivity. He needs to work on his relationship with Jesus. He needs quiet time working around the farm. I don't think he's getting much of that right now. You know what I mean?"

"I'll back off," I agreed. "But y'all know I love him. I'm worried about him, too. By all means, if it takes baseball and farm work and going to church and staying away from me to get him straight, fine. It's not like he's switching to Team Reason. At the same time, he's never going to be gullible enough to believe all the Noah's Ark, talking snakes, and Jonah getting swallowed by a whale kind of stuff. If y'all don't give him a little room to think and breathe, he's just gonna run in the opposite direction, maybe to some person y'all hate even more than me."

"A *fish*."

"What?"

"Jonah was in the belly of a *fish*."

"Ah, now *that* makes sense. Don't expect JD to buy those Bible fish stories hook, line, and sinker anymore. He's not a little boy. He's evolving. Oh, I forgot. You don't believe in evolution."

"I believe people can *de*volve. Quite frankly, I think I'm witnessing it right now."

"Go check on JD, Ronnie. But don't crucify him for blowing off a little steam or for doing the right thing on the baseball field. He's a good kid, and y'all know that."

As I turned and began walking down the hall toward the elevator, he simply said, "We're still praying for you, Ben."

"Cool," I responded as I gave a thumb's-up without turning. "Huge relief!"

* * *

When you leave a place like Possum Holler for an Ivy League school, go on to live and work in New York City, and marry a beautiful artsy woman with a British accent, folks back home think you've gotten too big for your britches, as my grandmother would have put it. Sure, when I first hit Wall Street, I briefly had a superiority complex, but I honestly shed that before I returned to Possum Holler. I met so many well-to-do idiots while living in New York that I gained a new respect in hindsight for some of the working poor folks of Possum Holler —the backyard mechanics, the pulp mill laborers, farmers, and others. Despite their Southern drawls and dirty clothes, they seemed to have had more common sense than most of the New Yorkers who restricted blood flow to their brains with neckties.

For the first few years back home, I gave the local folks the benefit of the doubt that—with the notable exceptions of some obvious local weirdos—they still possessed more wisdom per capita than city dwellers. Elizabeth and Riley didn't. They lumped all the Possum Holler and nearby folks into the same category—uneducated rubes whose worldviews came from Fox News and right-wing talk radio. To Elizabeth and Riley, New York was *their* "back home" where *they* thought most people were intelligent and cultured. Their leaving me didn't push me closer to their viewpoint, but I did begin to realize folks in Possum Holler were not the collective champions of common sense that my rose-colored retrospect glasses had made them out to be. Maybe the right wing had hijacked their brains en masse while I was up North. After all, half the restaurants, especially the barbecue joints, in the area had televisions that were tuned to Fox News, as if you could somehow stomach Laura Ingraham *and* pork at the same time. When I was growing up, few of those joints even played music, and only bars had televisions. Then again, maybe they seemed smarter back in the day because I was less worldly myself. Thank goodness for the soul food joints where I could wolf down delicious artery-clogging food while watching more educational shows like *Divorce Court* or *Family Feud*. If you wanted a restaurant without televised banality you had to drive an hour out of town to someplace really fancy, like Olive Garden in Warner Robins or Red Lobster in Albany. They might have televisions, too, but at least they'd be showing sporting events or those stupid sports shows where they yell at each other while debating such important issues as tush pushes and whether golfers and race car drivers qualify as *athletes*.

By that summer, I'd come to the opinion that I was one of the few people in Possum Holler, New York City or any point in between who had *any* common sense left. I realized Possum Holler and New York had the same amount of idiots, per capita, just different flavors. It could also be true that I had indeed gotten too big for my britches, figuratively speaking—OK, a little bit literally, too. At least in New York, I could look around the overgrown city and imagine that there must be another non-idiot out there somewhere. That was harder to imagine in Possum Holler where I was the proverbial big fish in a small, stagnant pond and knew nearly all the simple-minded minnows.

Immersed in twenty feet of Gulf water on this snorkeling excursion a day after JD headed home, I felt small for the first time in years. Struggling to navigate through fish and a boat wreck with my rented flippers, snorkel, and leaky mask was a salty reminder that I was insignificant in the grand scheme of things—even as the King of Possum Holler. I scanned the waters for bull sharks and zippy little sand sharks, but, much like the folks back home, none of the creatures were interested in me. It was depressing and reassuring at the same time. After fifteen minutes in the water, I noticed Jack was not spending much time under the surface.

"What's up?" I said as I broke the surface and removed my mask. "I've been trying to find the meaning of life down there but only got a couple of sand dollars."

"I'm worn out!" he said. "This is harder than it looks. But it's amazing even just looking down from the surface."

"Don't do a lot of snorkeling in New England, huh?"

"Did *you* snorkel in New York?"

"Yeah, found Jimmy Hoffa but ran out of breath. No, I get your point."

"But, hey, this is another educational experience," he said. "For all the negative stereotypes I've heard about the South, it has its treasures. And even the tiny handful of folks I've met have been pretty enlightening."

"Like JD?"

"He gives off that good ol' boy vibe at first, like you do, but he's got more layers—also like you. Of course, while you don't give a damn what anybody thinks, he *does*. The thought of disappointing people seems to really haunt him."

"Christian guilt. I see a lot of it back home. For what, though, who knows? The boy's about as straight-laced as they get these days. I don't think he's murdered hardly anybody. Can I ask you something, honestly?" I asked in all seriousness as I spit into my mask once again while bobbing in the waves.

"You wanna know if I'm gay?" he preempted me.

"What? That's pretty presumptive of you to think I'd ask something so personal? What kind of hick do you think I am?"

"The crazy kind, actually, but I'm sorry. Go on. What were you going to ask?"

"Are you *straight*?"

"If you must put a label on it—I don't—I guess I'm pansexual," he said quietly.

"Stay away from my kitchen then! You more into cast-iron, ceramic, what?"

"No, it means—" He stopped talking as I rolled my eyes. "Oh."

"I'm not a *total* hick, Jack. I *am* a hick, but I'm one who's seen a little bit of the world outside of Possum Holler. I know what the hell pansexual means."

"OK."

"Still, stay away from my blender. I've seen that thing crush some serious ice over the years."

# Ol' Henry's Foreboding Leg

Jack and I had plenty of time to chat on the way back to Possum Holler. In fact, we had *too much* time to talk. I liked the kid, but I still don't like *anybody* enough to talk for four hours straight. It's one of the reasons I stopped at Jackie's Family Restaurant in Donalsonville shortly after crossing the Georgia state line. Donalsonville is a small town famous for its proximity to the fishing hotspot of Lake Seminole and infamous for the horrific murders of six members of the Alday family in 1973. Jack looked warily at the nondescript concrete block building and its gravel parking lot.

"What's this?" he asked.

"Lunch. It's a meal Southerners have between breakfast and supper."

"Do you know this place?" he asked.

"Nope, never been."

"Maybe I'd better check Yelp first," he suggested.

"No need, kid. Let me school you on where to eat in a small Southern town. First, look for pickup trucks. If you see a bunch, that means they've got hearty food for workin' folks. It's a weekday, so these fellas are on their lunch breaks and need something hearty to get them through the rest of the day—and if they're *fat* workin' boys, all the better. Just ignore the rebel flags and bumper stickers about libtards and guns."

"Anything else?" he asked.

"Yeah, see who's coming out that door right now and that couple going in?"

"Old folks?" he said.

"Exactly! And they're regular old people, not some fancy-pants folks from Atlanta who eat at restaurants for the *ambiance*. They're here because they are getting a lot of bang for their buck. Now, check the license plates."

"All Georgia?" he noted.

"More specific?"

"Um, ok, Seminole, Seminole, Seminole—"

"Seminole County. *Local* folks. This is where the locals eat. You can't have a crappy restaurant in a small town and draw a crowd for very long. So, it's hearty, it's affordable, and it must be pretty good. Trust me, kid. When it comes to delicious, artery-clogging food at an affordable price, I know what I'm talking about."

"Generalize much?"

"Some stereotypes are *generally* true," I said.

"But *you* don't fit all the Southern stereotypes."

"Every rule has an exception, and I'm an exception to damn near every rule. I'm special. At least, that's what my mama said when she put me on the bus. I'm the roasted cauliflower you won't find in this joint. Now, let's eat. You can Yelp it afterward, right after you thank me."

Sure enough, Jackie's Family Restaurant notched another five-star Yelp review that day with special recognition given to the peach cobbler on the all-you-can-eat buffet. Better still, Jack asked if he could lie down in the back seat of the truck to nap on the way home. All out of words, I enthusiastically approved. I tuned to smooth jazz on the radio—yes, it's a preset just like JD said—and the only other things I heard on the way home were the hum of the tires on the blacktop and the sounds of Jack getting fatter by the mile, making room for it all with an occasional fart—girly poots, really, but still potent.

* * *

The silence of my kingdom was deafening the next few days. I got a single text from JD that he was back home but would not be dropping by for a little while. Jack spent his mornings and afternoons "researching" as he visited such sites as Andersonville National Historic Site and the Jimmy Carter stuff in nearby Plains. He would have an early dinner each night in the towns within fifteen miles of Possum Holler—a barbecue joint in Oglethorpe, a pizza place in Americus, and a cafeteria-style restaurant run by Mennonites just outside of Montezuma. He would then spend the rest of the night writing—or so he said. If he was indeed penning some *Gone with the Fried Green Crawdads* indictment of the South, he had plenty of material to work with. I suspected that he would sum up the South as "a nice place to eat, but I wouldn't want to live there." If I could think of one, I'd offer a forceful rebuttal.

Meanwhile, I was unemployed and bored with managing my investments online. How the hell did I ever do this shit every day for a living? With Jack doing his own thing, JD out of sight, Riley continuing to ignore my texts and emails, I realized that I was not immune to loneliness. Sure, I possessed some loner tendencies—still do—and *choosing* to be a loner is freeing. Being forced into it, however, feels more like solitary confinement. I decided to take a vacation in my own backyard, blasting tropical music and mixing fruity drinks to put in the cupholder of my inflatable pool lounger, but I couldn't fool myself. I was floating in circles, literally and figuratively. By Friday, a week after our return from the Redneck Riviera, I'd had enough alone time. I saw Jack's car still in the driveway for a change, so I knocked on the door.

"I'm going into town to grab some Samburgers," I said. "You want some?"

"Some?"

"Yeah, best burgers on the planet. Little sliders like White Castle or Krystal but way better. Faster, too."

"I guess so. Am I dressed OK?" He was barefoot and wearing his Red Sox T-shirt and exercise shorts.

"Well, Sam's Snack Shack ain't exactly Le Bernardin, but you might wanna at least put on some flip-flops."

"I don't own flip-flops."

"Good grief. Well, put on some sneakers, mister fancy pants, and let's go."

Tucked away on a side street in downtown Montezuma, Sam's Snack Shack was older than I and far more popular. A block away from the famous joint, I told Jack to roll down the passenger window.

"You mean *let* it down? Why?"

"Geez. I forget how young you are. Just do it."

"Wow, what's that smell?"

"Sam's."

"Smells like grease," he said.

"You're welcome. I believe we've covered this in a previous lesson in Florida."

We parked at the far end of Maple Street and walked the sidewalk past the several vacant storefronts with broken windows and posters for church events that had happened months earlier before pausing where Ms. Cordelia had set up a table to sell baked goods. After moving back home, I never went to Sam's without stopping for a bag of her cookies.

"Hey, baby," she greeted me. "How y'all doin' today?"

"Nothing but fine," I replied.

"I got chocolate chips and oatmeal-raisin?"

"Ms. Cordelia, you know I want chocolate chip. I'll get 'em on the way back, though. I don't want to spoil my lunch."

"OK, baby. I'll save this bag for you."

It was 11:45 a.m., and the crowd waiting to order already spilled through the swinging screen door to Sam's. Two lines of hungry folks jockeyed for position, stepping aside every few seconds to let other patrons exit with their full brown bags dripping grease.

"Looks healthy," Jack noted with a grin.

"I can take you to get a salad somewhere if you prefer," I said.

"Well, since we're already here...What are *you* getting?"

"They've got fried chicken, but it's against my religion to get fried chicken from a burger joint or burgers from a chicken joint."

"So, you're getting—?"

"Three double-chili-cheese *without*, fries, and a Diet Coke," I blurted in less than two seconds.

"Wow, that was almost robotic."

"Probably because it's the same thing I ordered the last 847 times."

"What does *without* mean?" he asked.

"Onions. They've got these little yellow onions that will knock you out of your seat. Too much for me. You can get yours *all the way* if you want. Most folks do."

"What's *all the way* mean?"

"*With* onions."

"Oh, well, I'll take two double-cheeseburgers *all the way* and fries with a regular Coke," he said.

"Are you trying to kill yourself? I'm not buying that diabetes in a bottle. You're having Diet Coke. Besides, it offsets the cholesterol and fat. Don't look at me like that. It's science."

It took four minutes to go from outside the door to the front of the line—seemed like a damn lifetime. I placed our order as Jack watched the operation in amazement. The cook, Sam, a grumpy old fellow who never took the orders, simply flipped burgers and doused them with sauce, adding onions and cheese to some as his skinny brother who took the orders shouted, "Two double-cheese all the way! Three double-chili-cheese without!" That was followed by the heavily tattooed and oft-pierced girl taking others' orders shouting, "Four chili-cheese without! Two chili-cheese-slaw dogs all the way! One chicken breast!" Sam never looked up, and the barked orders never stopped. The skinny fellow threw our burgers in a bag, followed by a couple of fries. He then slapped two Diet Cokes on the counter.

"Damn, that was fast!" Jack observed.

"A little slow today. Sixty-five seconds. Somebody must have the day off."

"Are we going back to the house to eat them?" Jack asked as he looked around the crowded joint with its lines still stretching out the door and jam-packed booths and tables.

"You can't make your first Samburger *to go*. You gotta eat it while the grease is still hot. Plus, you gotta soak up the ambiance. Follow me, rookie."

I weaved through the loyal patrons to the table farthest back with just one other patron sitting there, an elderly black man we all knew only as Ol' Henry. He spent his afternoons sitting on a bench on Dooly Street waving at passing vehicles but spent most of his mornings at Sam's, where he'd order a sausage biscuit and coffee and camp out at that table for a few hours. Most folks avoided him because he was known for lying about everything—his age, how he lost his leg, where he was from, you name it. I found his fibs refreshing compared to folks who pretended to be things they were most definitely not, such as those who attended church religiously on Sunday—pun intended.

"Mind if we join you, Henry?" I asked as I slid into the booth opposite the table, followed by Jack. "This is Jack. He's visiting from Boston."

"Boston?" Henry asked. "Down there around Thomasville, right?"

"Massachusetts, actually," Jack corrected.

"Jack doesn't know all the big cities here in Georgia," I said. "He doesn't realize you can tour the world right here in Georgia.

We've got Rome, Athens, Cairo, Dublin, Vienna, Damascus, and, of course, Boston, which is about as big as Possum Holler. How you doing today, Henry?"

"My leg's killin' me!" he said. "Does it every time storms are rollin' in."

"Where the gator bit it off?" I asked.

"Naw, below that—down where it got machine-gunned off by the Germans. Ambushed in Tunisia, 1943. I carried that leg in one arm and shot the rest with my other."

"If you don't mind my asking, how old are you?" Jack asked, followed by, "Oh my God, these are delicious!"

"A hunnerd'n twenty-six!" Henry announced proudly. "Let me hold a French fry."

I put a paper towel on the table and shook out several fries. "Least I can do to thank you for your service—and to celebrate your record."

"What record?" Henry asked.

"World's oldest person. That's impressive. You oughta call the Guinness Book of World Records."

"They ain't puttin' no black man in that book. They only put old Japanese folks in there and talk about how they 115 years old and drinking whiskey and smoking cigars every day. Bullshit."

"Well," I said as I lifted my first double-chili-cheeseburger *without* as if it were a glass of champagne, "here's to living longer than we should. I probably should've bit the dust years ago. Almost did with a heart attack a few years ago."

"How old are you?" Henry asked.

"Fifty-one."

"You just a baby!" he said with a laugh before asking Jack, "How old are you?"

"Eighteen," he responded.

"I thought you were at least nineteen," I said. "You've been in college for a year."

"Yeah, but my birthday's in October, so I guess it was up to my parents when to start me in school. They started me early."

"Just the opposite of JD," I said. "His birthday's in October, too, but they didn't want to rush him." I then noticed Henry grimace. Whether it was the handiwork of the gator or the Germans, he was clearly experiencing phantom pains in his missing leg.

"Storms huh?" I asked.

"Yeah, somethin' bad coming. It always aches when rain's comin', but when it hurts like this, damn, it must be a hurricane out there."

"Well, we're two hundred miles from the beach, so that should keep the storm surge manageable," I said.

A huge clap of thunder shook the building.

"Goddamn, Germans!" Henry yelled.

Jack and I wolfed down our Samburgers, but we couldn't get out of Sam's before the rain began pounding against the plate-glass windows. Ms. Cordelia had packed up her cookies and departed before we made our run to the truck. There was going to be a problem, however, if I tried to operate the windshield wipers. That sweet old lady had left a plastic bag of chocolate chip cookies under the driver's side wiper blade. I was going to have to pay her double on my next Sam's run.

"Here," I said as I tossed the little bag of cookies into Jack's lap. "Between Samburgers and these cookies, trust me: You may never want to go back to Boston."

"I may be too fat to fit in my car to go back to Boston."

"Yeah, you've got to be pushing 140 pounds by now. Maybe we can call you Fat Jack in a few weeks. Once you start going by two names, you'll be officially Southern."

"But *you* only go by one name, Ben."

"I'm *unofficially* Southern. Once you leave and get too big for your britches—literally in your case—you can never be *official* again."

By the time we made it to my driveway, massive rain blobs had given way to hail pellets. Jack hopped out of the passenger side and looked nervously toward the west, where the sky was darkening.

"Should we take cover?" he yelled over the racket caused by the ice hitting the truck.

"*You* might want to," I said.

"Where are you going?"

"To get my camera in case a tornado pops up. There have been at least ten tornadoes around Possum Holler in my lifetime, and I ain't seen a damn one of 'em. I was either a few miles off or a few states off."

"Isn't that a little dangerous?" Jack asked.

"It's a *lot* dangerous, but what's the worst that could happen?"

"Um, you get blown into a field, parts of you get blown into a field, a tree falls on you, you get hit by a flying cow—"

"I'm *moo*ved by your concern, but I'll take my chances. If you see two guys in a rowboat fly by, though, let me know. I can't handle landing in any weird land run by munchkins. That *Lollipop Guild* has freaked me out for a half-century now."

"I'm more worried about the Winkies," Jack said.

"Well, it's not unusual to get the winkies after a couple of Samburgers. But that's perfectly natural—and worth it."

"What? Never mind. *I'll* be in here. Enjoy the storm," Jack said while peeking his head out of the door to his apartment. He shut it just as my phone blared a severe thunderstorm warning from the National Weather Service.

"Well, I'll be damned," I said to myself. "Ol' Henry's leg was right. Hell, maybe he *is* 126."

Pine trees bent nearly to their breaking points as the wind accelerated and the sky darkened further. I wasn't joking about never having seen a tornado. I ran to the bedroom and grabbed my Canon Rebel. I'm no photographer, but I had purchased a good bit of camera gear and paraphernalia through the years as I documented Riley's younger days, back when she still loved me. Those photos depicted a happy, smiling daddy's girl that Riley claimed she didn't remember, though I rarely mustered the courage to gaze upon the pictures through the tears that inevitably welled up in my eyes. Doing so would trigger blurry replays in my mind and send my brain spiraling into insane loops of wondering to which year I would return if I could time travel and correct the choices that had stranded me in Possum Holler. I certainly would have gone back and slapped some sense into me when I first got the notion to move Elizabeth and Riley to Georgia. It may have once been home to me, but it was never much more than a prison to Elizabeth or Riley.

With no time to grab the tripod, I rushed to the back deck and pressed my back against the door of the house to avoid the ice pellets that had become wind-driven bullets. Then I heard what sounded like—I couldn't believe what I was thinking—a freight train. I swear to y'all's God, those folks interviewed by TV news were right—*it sounded like a damn freight train*. There was a good reason for what I heard, though—an *actual* freight train on the nearby tracks. It was heading north into the darkest part of the storm. *Ding!* A tornado warning popped up on my phone. I scanned the wet sky but saw no funnel clouds. I then heard what sounded like the world's largest aluminum cans being crushed. Thuds and clangs of something being destroyed echoed through the entire holler, followed by an extended, deep-bass rumbling.

"Oh shit," I whispered to myself. "I hope it didn't take out the trestles over Timber Creek before the train got there."

* * *

Winds eventually gave way to a light breeze. The familiar smell of fresh-cut pines wafted over my kingdom, but Mother Nature was the lumberjack this time. I pounded on Jack's door.

"Everything all right?" he asked.

"I don't know. Sounded like a tornado, but of course I didn't see it. Get on something you don't mind getting dirty and be in the truck in five minutes."

I fueled up the chainsaw and tossed it in the back of the pickup along with my disorganized bag of random tools. Jack barely had time to shut the passenger door before I sped up my muddy driveway toward 228, my tires splattering the silver sides of my truck with orange dots. With the rain down to a sprinkle, I saw little damage to any of the farmhouses and outbuildings over the first couple of miles. By the third mile, the snapped trees had gone from a few to many.

Jack seized the oh-shit handle as I yanked the wheel hard to the left at the intersection of 228 and Bailey Road, which was paved to the right but dirt to the left.

"Where are we going?" Jack asked as his knuckles turned white on the oh-shit handle.

"Bailey compound."

"Compound?"

"Yeah, several families living in a couple of old houses and several trailers. Been there for generations, but they're kind of stuck there because their grandparents and great-grandparents wanted to make sure white folks wouldn't steal the land from their kids, so they deeded it so that they can only sell to other family members."

"Makes sense," Jack said.

"Well, I'm sure their intentions were good, but it robbed their future generations of their equity and mobility. Hence, they're stuck."

As we neared the Baileys' four-acre pecan orchard, I saw dozens of limbs on the ground and several trees uprooted. I knew the land well because Travis Bailey and I had been classmates from kindergarten through senior year. We'd played youth league basketball, baseball, and football both together and against each other before high school. I got to know him especially well during a couple of years in the early eighties when his grandmother would babysit me for a couple of hours after school when my mother had gone back to work as a secretary while my father's well-digging business slumped just before he got a steadier job at the new pulp mill. Travis and I would ride the bus back to his grandmother's old house that not only had a tin roof but also gaudy blue tin siding. It made a heck of a ruckus when it rained. Between that house and Travis' family's white concrete block home was once a patch of dirt with a rotting plywood backboard nailed to a tree and a bent goal with a few strands of string where a net had once been. I liked to think that's where I helped make Travis a high school basketball star because I boosted his confidence through the afternoon beat-downs he gave me—beatdowns that likely inspired me to try sports like tennis where there were no Travises to contend with. Travis would go on to excel in prep hoops as a 6-foot-3 power forward, but didn't have the size to compete at similar positions at the collegiate level, not that his grades would have allowed it. While my tennis skills weren't quite enough to take me to the college level, I did land that academic scholarship to Brown. I think our academic and athletic departures had a lot to do with our drifting apart after middle school. Besides, close friendships between blacks and whites back then garnered a side-eye from many local folks—from *both* races. You could have friends from other races, but not to the extent that they were invited to sleepovers and such. It probably didn't make Travis feel any better that his grandmother, Ms. Ruby, worked daily for the white Chatham family down the road for what I suspect was inadequate, cash-only pay for demeaning tasks. I hadn't seen him in at least a year, not since we bumped into each other at The Party Shop liquor store in nearby Oglethorpe. He was drunk, but he remembered me, and I recognized him despite the extra hundred pounds he had put on over the years. We shook hands, and he asked if I knew of any jobs around. I said no. That was the end of the conversation. There was no reminiscing.

As we rounded the corner of the orchard, I could see that the home where Travis grew up and now lived was still standing, but there was a hole in the roof, and a couple of windows were shattered. The basketball backboard was gone, likely having rotted completely away decades earlier, much like his dreams of hoops stardom.

The late Ms. Ruby's home was a crumpled heap of tin, and three mobile homes that had been added on the other side of her house had been reduced to splinters and pieces of yellow insulation that also were strewn across the land. A flimsy wooden rectangular church the family built decades earlier was intact a few dozen yards beyond those with the exception of a steeple that I could have sworn was there when I was a child. Across a pasture in which several cows milled about as if nothing had happened were two of the older stick-built homes with tin roofs that appeared to have been spared.

We jumped out of the truck and ran to join family members sorting through the wreckage of the mobile homes and the remains of Ms. Ruby's house. Family members were hugging and crying, and some reached toward the sky to thank the Lord for their lives. Most of the family was not on the property because it was a weekday. A scream pierced the gray drizzle. It came from Travis' house.

Everyone ran toward his rickety front porch steps but stopped in the yard. Travis walked slowly through a front screen door that was held on by a single hinge. In his arms was a toddler. Blood trickled from his forehead. The girl was lifeless. The tortured face that had just let out that scream appeared equally so. He shook his head back and forth as he looked toward the damp, gray sky.

"Imani!" he screamed as he fell to his knees on the porch with this little girl's feet dangling off of one arm and her head drooped over the other. Extended family huddled around him, some placing their arms upon his shoulders while others stretched their arms toward the heavens.

"Let's give 'em space," I told Jack. I dialed 9-1-1 as we quietly walked toward the truck. The 9-1-1 operator sounded frazzled.

"Yeah, I'm at the Bailey place on Bailey Road near 228. I believe the storm killed a little girl out here."

"We're sending help now."

I told a couple of extended family members that emergency services had been summoned, then motioned for Jack to get into the truck.

"Where are we going?" he asked.

"Gotta check on JD and my sister," I said quietly.

They lived a couple of miles east of the Bailey place, which potentially placed them in the path of the tornado. The tornado, though, had veered more to the northeast and fizzled out in the cornfields near Oglethorpe. When I saw my sister's home and their church were untouched by the storm, I didn't stop. I was in no frame of mind to deal with my sister or Ronnie. I'd never seen a dead child before that day. That night, I cried and drank straight tequila on my back deck, alone. I'd lost Riley, but not in the same way the Baileys had lost that little girl. I couldn't imagine the grief, as bad as my own seemed. Yet, so long as I lived on the same Earth as Riley, I would not give up the tiny spark of hope that she and I would patch things up in a year or two or twenty. They didn't even have that dying ember. The image of the Baileys rallying around each other in the wake of the tragedy haunted me. They had family and faith to lean on. I had nothing. I sincerely wished I believed in something besides the Gospel according to Jimmy Buffett. But I didn't, and I knew pretending to believe would do me no good. I wouldn't buy my performance. Perhaps worst of all, I didn't even believe in myself. I drank with the intention of passing out on the back deck. I succeeded.

* * *

Imani was just two years old and was Travis' granddaughter. Her mother, Shantae, Travis' daughter, waitressed full-time at the Waffle House in Americus and worked part-time on the maintenance staff at Muckalee Christian. She would politely smile at me when we passed in the halls. I tried to engage her in conversation or at least exchange pleasantries, but she always acted busy. I think she was embarrassed to be cleaning up after a bunch of white kids, many of them spoiled in her eyes. She was pulling a shift at the Waffle House the day the tornado came and had no idea what was happening fifteen miles north. Imani's father was an Army soldier stationed in Germany. He never married Shantae and was not close to the family. Imani was killed by pieces of the family's rickety church on the compound, including the steeple that had crashed through her bedroom window and ceiling.

I attended the funeral a week later under a large funeral home tent that was temporarily erected by a local funeral home on the Bailey property. I stood quietly in the back. There was nothing I could do to comfort the family, especially wailing Travis and Shantae, who at one point staggered to her feet and collapsed onto the small casket. I had been to several white folks' funerals through the years in and around Possum Holler. There was no wailing at any of them, just folks sobbing and quietly dabbing away at tears. Maybe the intense displays of emotion were a black thing, and I wasn't meant to understand. Then again, I had never been to any funeral for a child. Even the reserved Baptists, Methodists, and Free-Willers I'd known through the years might've reacted similarly under the same circumstances.

More than two hundred people attended Imani's funeral that day. Only one attendee was white.

# The Blessing

The National Weather Service rated it a "minor" EF-1 tornado. The Bailey family thought it was pretty goddamn major. The storm didn't even make the Montezuma weekly paper's front page. My nightmares about struggling to connect with Riley began to feature disturbing appearances by little Imani. I continued to sip the days away by the pool and guzzled the nights away on the deck. I was more lost than ever before, and I was fully aware of it. I wasn't drifting aimlessly. I was a stationary, unmotivated blob with nothing to offer the world, not even historical facts and context for otherwise indoctrinated private school kids.

Jack quietly did his research and laid low. He certainly had plenty of material for his journal. He had a little more than three weeks to go in the apartment. Certainly, they couldn't be as eventful as the first few.

A few days after the funeral, my phone rang. It was my beloved sister, though it had been so long since she had called me that it took a moment to remember who "Sis" was on the display. It was after 5 p.m., and I was buzzing pretty good. I didn't want to answer, but I did just in case it was news about JD.

"Hey, Sis. How's JD?"

"Why thank you, I'm fine," she said. "And JD's good."

"What's up?"

"Ronnie and I have been praying and talking, and we believe in the power of forgiveness—and the importance of family. I know my younger days were a little wild, but they were wasted. I was able to turn it all around, and life is beautiful."

"Well, I'm happy for you."

"There's still time for you, Ben."

"I'm afraid *my* time has already slipped through my fingers, Sis," I said before offering a small dose of contrition. "Look, I really am sorry about what happened with JD. We may have our differences, but he's your son. And Ronnie's. I overstepped. I admit it. He's a good kid, and I ain't exactly a role model for anybody right now. Y'all were absolutely right."

"Look," she said. "I realized while we were hiding in the basement after the tornado warning that family is worth fighting for. You're my brother, and, believe it or not, I love you. And, yeah, you are a terrible role model, but JD loves you, too. We're family no matter what. And you *can* change."

"I care about y'all, too, and I'm sorry we have nothing in common."

"We don't have to. We're family. We're...we're blood. Right?"

"Yeah."

"I want y'all to come to dinner Saturday night," she said. "A good, old-fashioned country supper."

“Y’all?”

“Yes, JD wants to invite that kid staying with you.”

“Jack?”

“Yes. He said he’s a good kid and smart and they had a lot in common and that I shouldn’t hold whatever anger I had for you against him.”

“Well, that makes sense. They definitely have a lot in common. And I do think he’s a decent fellow—for a Yankee anyway.”

“You and I have both been Yankees at some point, too,” she said with a chuckle.

“Temporary Yankee don’t count.”

“Oh, OK. Y’all be there Saturday at six o’clock.”

“I think I have an Optimist Club meeting at six,” I argued.

“See y’all at six.”

“Taylor Swift Fan Club meeting?”

“Six.”

At least that call was less combative than our previous one. Why the hell do we have to do dinner, though? Hadn’t I suffered enough? Hadn’t we *all* suffered enough? “Geez,” I muttered to myself, who readily agreed with me.

* * *

Jack eagerly accepted the dinner invitation. Maybe he was just tired of local joints and leftover pizza slices. Perhaps he had witnessed enough of local folks like me who did not fit in and wanted to understand folks who *did* fit perfectly in Possum Holler. He wore the same white, long-sleeved shirt and khakis in which he first arrived in Possum Holler. I wore formal wear—one of my nicer pairs of cargo shorts and a Braves T-shirt.

I properly introduced Jack to Ronnie and Sarah, and they invited us into their living room. My sister had the decorating taste of a classy old Southern lady even though she was just a couple years older than me. The images of her teenage bedroom in our house with its posters of heavy metal bands covering the walls were a far cry from this living room of pillows, throws, and all kinds of fragile vases, china, and what-nots and do-dads. Jack looked around as if he had just strolled into a gift shop at a *Gone with the Wind* museum.

We sat and chatted like old folks while JD remained outside on their back porch manning the grill. Actually, *they* chatted with Jack while I quietly listened to the questioning and the tick-tock of their grandfather clock. I felt like an intruder, as I always did in that house, but Jack seemed right at home.

"You look familiar," Sarah said.

Ronnie nodded and looked at Jack as if he were there for a job interview. It made *me* uncomfortable. I was used to being judged by Ronnie but not seeing others subjected to it.

"Well, y'all just saw him in Panama City," I explained.

"Yes, for a second," Sarah retorted. "That's not what I mean."

"Y'all don't start," Ronnie warned. "What's your story, son?"

Jack explained that he was an only child, another thing he had in common with JD. He had done well in grade school and was accepted into a prestigious boarding school in nearby Groton before receiving an academic scholarship to Boston U. He mentioned again that he was fascinated by sociology and that he was down South to observe, listen and learn. When they asked what he thought about the South so far, he said that the pace of life was refreshingly slower than in Boston, though he noted that his perspective might be different had he been staying in Atlanta instead of Possum Holler.

"Anything in particular strike you as different?" Ronnie asked.

"The food, wow, absolutely amazing!" he said. "I'm definitely going to have to join a gym when I get back home."

"Totally understand," Ronnie said with a chuckle. "I actually grew up in Connecticut. I was a little skinnier then." Sis smiled. "OK, I was a *lot* skinnier then. Sarah and I actually met in New York while my band was trying to make it."

"What'd you play?" Jack asked.

"Rhythm guitar and backup vocals, believe it or not," Ronnie said as he glanced down upon the coffee table with a brief wistful smile. "I was a different person then."

"How come y'all never told me this?" I asked. "I thought you were always a preacher man."

"People change, Ben," Sis said, "sometimes, for the better." She grabbed Ronnie's hand and gave it a squeeze. "I know I did."

"We both did, darlin'," he responded.

"That's interesting," Jack said.

I wanted to know more about this rockin' revelation, but JD kept coming in and out through the screen door in the nearby kitchen, and the grill smoke was creeping into the room and my nostrils.

"What's JD grilling out there?" I interrupted.

"Dry-rubbed ribs and smoked sausage," Ronnie said as he stood up. "Oughta be about done. Y'all come get something to drink and find a spot at the table. Jack, you want sweet tea or homemade lemonade?"

"Lemonade sounds great, sir," Jack responded.

"Ugh," I muttered over his calling Ronnie "sir." It sounded a little Eddie Haskel-ish.

"Ben, lemonade or sweet tea?"

"Well, I could definitely use a drink. I guess lemonade'll do. Only one shot of tequila, though. I gotta drive."

Neither Sarah nor Ronnie acknowledged my jab at their teetotaling ways. We walked to the dining room, where Sarah had two full crystal pitchers ready on the long farmhouse wood table, and five glasses of melting ice were distributed evenly.

"So, Jack, you have a church up there in Boston?" Sarah asked as she poured the lemonade.

"No, ma'am. My dad is Jewish...well, by ancestry anyway. He's not observant. My mom was raised Presbyterian, but they haven't been to church in years. I've only been in a few churches myself—weddings and such."

"You should join us tomorrow." I'd warned Jack this moment was coming. I glanced at him and caught his eye to remind him that he was in no way obligated to accept the invitation. He abruptly broke eye contact with me.

"I'd love to."

"I'm sorry, what?" I interjected.

"You're welcome, too, Ben, as always" Ronnie said as he emerged from the back porch with a pan full of ribs and JD following closely behind with a plate full of smoked sausage. "I promise to not preach about Jonah and the fish—even though I know how much you like that one," he added with a smirk. "Actually, we're going New Testament tomorrow, as you say you prefer, with the second greatest commandment."

"Ah, love thy neighbor," I noted. "I didn't know Christians still listened to Jesus." JD tried unsuccessfully to suppress a chuckle. Jack took his seat quietly, seeming to hope he could push us closer to dinner and farther from any family drama.

"Actually," Ronnie said, "I don't want to hurt your feelings, Ben, but I kind of agree with you. We *do* spend too much time on the Old Testament and not enough on the New. So what do you say?"

"About agreeing on something? Yeah, it is a little disturbing."

"No, about joining us at church tomorrow. You don't have to sing any hymns or even talk to anyone. You can sit in the back quietly and just enjoy Sunday morning worship."

"I appreciate the invite, but I don't go anywhere I have to wear a tie. Never again. I mean, it'd be different if they held your head on or something, but they're just neck decorators. What's the point? It's the dumbest invention in history."

"Wow, it *has* been a long time since you've gone to church, hasn't it?" Sis chimed in. "Actually, very few men wear ties to church these days, Ben."

"Except for me," Ronnie added with a laugh. "I'm afraid we preachers are still expected to have—what'd you call 'em—neck decorators?"

JD plopped down in the chair directly across from Jack, and the boys stared at me. God, it's aggravating to get scolding looks from teenagers. I guess it really is hard to raise an uncle.

"All right, all right—I'll *think* about it," I said. It was a lie. I just wanted to get on with dinner and speed up my exit.

"Well, I'll give you a good reason to go tomorrow if you're looking for one," Ronnie said.

"Wouldn't *hurt* to have a good reason."

"Whatever you think about the church and religion, it *does* have the power to marshal resources for good in ways that secular organizations just can't," he said. "For instance, tomorrow after church, the Riverside Men—the men's ministry—are gathering in the parking lot to assemble a bunch of 2-by-4s into walls that are going to a nonprofit building a house for a family in need. They'll put the walls on a truck and haul them to the build site where some other volunteers will stand them up. Gives their project a big head start, and they're planning to build the home in one week. We do it every summer. Whaddya think?"

"I've heard about it from JD, yes, and I think it's great," I said. "I like to see churches doing good stuff."

"Join us."

"Can't I just come for the wall building part?" I asked.

"Well, it's really kind of a way to tie what we hear *inside* the church to what we do *outside* the church, and it's also to strengthen bonds among the men of the church," Ronnie said. "It's a unity thing. And the women's group is serving us lunch before we kick off the build. One hour of church won't kill you, I promise."

"OK, I'll think about it. Honest."

"Well, will miracles never cease?" Sis chimed in with a smile. "Now, let's eat. Everybody, bow your heads. You don't have to if you don't want, Jack."

"Thank you, but I'll bow."

I also bowed. I had been a nonbeliever living among Christians and working in a Christian school for the past several years, so prayers were no big deal to me. Granted, I often had to overlook some of the things for which they either gave credit to God or stuff they asked of the big guy. I'd roll my eyes *under* my eyelids, which made me feel better, and no one had to know. Besides, it allowed me a moment to reflect however I wanted while the Christians spoke to the sky. I rather enjoyed the invocation before home football games at Muckalee Christian when the public address announcer, Mr. Hyder, would ask God to protect the kids from injury as they hurled their bodies against each other and then end each prayer with some gentle humor: "...and may the losing team have a safe trip home. Amen."

"Heavenly father," Sarah began. "We are thankful to be gathered today with family and new friends. We give thanks again for your loving and protective hands that saved JD from serious injury recently and kept our family, our home and our church safe from the tornado. We pray for safety again tomorrow as we put faith into action, shining your divine light *outside* the church and *into* our community. We ask that you bless this food to the nourishment of our bodies. In Jesus' name we pray, amen."

"He certainly answered our prayers the other day," Ronnie said as the boys began attacking the food on their plates as if they had just been rescued from a deserted island.

"God is good *all* the time," Sis said, giving a nod toward the fully healed JD.

As silverware clanged against my dinner mates' plates, I sat motionless and stared down at my plate. The food looked delicious, and I was starving. Yet, I feared that if I took a single bite, I'd throw up.

"Something wrong?" Sis asked when she noticed I had yet to begin eating.

"I can't do it," I said matter-of-factly.

"Excuse me," Sis angrily responded.

"God is good *all the time*?" I repeated. "*All* the time? A little girl *died* in that tornado, just a few miles thataway. Two years old. *Two years old*! And you think God killed *her* and saved *y'all*? Why? Because she was from a poor black family? You're giving God credit for saving y'all and killing that little girl."

"I blame God for nothing!" Sis yelled. "It's all part of His plan. And don't you *dare* come into my home and accuse me of being racist!"

"I'm just saying that if he gets *credit* for saving y'all, he should get the *blame* for killing that little girl. God's got one hell of a sweet gig—all of the credit and none of the blame! If God had a job review, they'd put him on probation and consider promoting Satan. Or, hell, I'll take it. I'm jobless, and I haven't killed *anybody*."

"What you don't understand—well, one of the many *many* things you don't get—is that little girl is lucky," Sis insisted. "God made her an angel that day. She is in His loving arms now, and we should all be so lucky."

JD and Jack nervously whispered back and forth.

"Well, he could have made her an angel in a hell of a less violent way! Why all of the hullabaloo? By the way, that little girl was literally crushed by the cross from the steeple of that family's little church. I guess religion continues to be the undisputed champion of killing people for no good reason."

"You can go now, Ben," Ronnie said solemnly before taking a sip of water and then calmly placing it back onto the table. As much as I despised his philosophy, I did admire his ability to keep cool in any situation. Perhaps when God wasn't out striking down little girls with tornado-hurled crosses, he found time to grant Ronnie the kind of inner peace I longed for.

"Gladly. Thank y'all for the almost dinner. Jack?"

"I'll give him a ride home after dinner," JD said.

"Wow," I said as I glanced disapprovingly toward Jack. "Church and now dinner with the fam? Hey, it's *your* story. I can't wait to read it. By the way, at church tomorrow, if you see any black folks there, be sure to tell 'em I said 'hey.'"

Jack stared at me blankly. I thought I knew the kid. Then again, he had not been in Possum Holler long enough to be much more than a stranger to me. It was almost as if he were *trying* to fit in with this family rather than simply observe and understand. I *lived* in Possum Holler. I *grew up* in Possum Holler, and I didn't even want to fit in. Why the hell did Jack care about these folks?

# The Finger

While Jack was enjoying what no doubt was a delicious dinner with Sis and family, I microwaved two potentially expired wieners and wrapped each in a piece of white bread with mustard and ketchup. For dessert, I had a gummy and put my mind to rest. When those gummies kicked in, even the most troubling thoughts that regularly invaded my mind were held at bay for a little while. Granted, they induced wild dreams that I had trouble remembering in the mornings—recalling only the sense of dread that haunted me afterward.

While Jack was learning about the Lord the next morning with his best bud JD, I cranked up the blender early in a quest to be good and buzzed by the time the Braves game started. I was damn near passed out drunk on my pool float when a sweat-drenched Jack moped from his car to the apartment door.

"Hey, Bob Vila!" I yelled. "How'd it go?"

"Wow, JD was right—you really do need some references from the twenty-first century."

"I'd call you one of those tall twin dudes that renovate crap, but I don't know their names. You know, the guy married to the doe-eyed chick from *Elf*. That better? So, how'd it go?"

"Service was fine, I guess," he said as he walked toward the pool. "It's not really my thing—the hymns and sermon and praying and stuff. But I did enjoy the lunch and the fellowship. I can see why people are attracted to it."

"And the wall-building thing?"

"I hit a few nails—missed a few more. Guess I'm no Bob Vila. They're putting the walls on a truck now and taking them someplace in Alabama."

"What? I thought they were doing it for a local home," I said.

"Nah, it's someplace a few hours away."

"I thought Ronnie was going to be preaching some of that 'Love thy neighbor' shit. We've got neighbors down the road who just got hit by a damn tornado. You recall that day, right?"

"Yes, and that's why JD and I suggested the men's group get together again Saturday morning and go out there," Jack said.

"Well, I'll be damned," I said. "And here I was ready to give up on you. What a decent *Christian* you're turning out to be. There are so few of you left."

"I detect sarcasm."

"Nah, I'm actually OK with that faith-in-action stuff. I just don't see much of it from church folks around here—a lot more talking the talk than walking the walk."

"Do you want to?"

"Want to what?"

"See it in action."

"Sure."

"I was hoping you'd say that," he said. "None of us really know the family. But you do. Any chance you could drop by there and see how we can help?"

"Um, I'm a bit inebriated at the moment."

"How's that different from other moments?"

He had a point. Lying around drunk in a pool was not exactly making the world a better place. I could not sit back and cast stones at the Christians if I wasn't doing anybody any good my own damn self.

"Fine," I said. "I'll give Travis a holler later and see if we can help."

"See, I told them they were wrong about you being an asshole," he said.

"You shouldn't bear false witness at church, you know."

"Can I be straight with you for a second?" he asked.

"I thought you were pansexual," I said.

"Seriously."

"K, go ahead."

"JD's worried about you." I leaned back on the float and stared at the clouds. "Now that you're not teaching, I think he worries you don't have anything positive to focus on—and he feels like he's kinda responsible, you know, after that day on the baseball field. He feels guilty."

"You can't have a healthy religion without a heaping dose of guilt, but it's not his fault," I said. "But, yeah, he's right. I ain't got a whole lot of positive shit to hang on to at the moment in case you haven't noticed. No job. My daughter hates me. No wife. No family. No purpose. I've lost everything that made me *me*."

"Don't give up hope," he said. "That's the one thing none of us can live without."

"OK, Dr. Phil, I'll give it a shot," I said as I paddled my float toward the pool stairs. "Speaking of which, I need another drink."

"You mean you *want* another drink."

"Jesus! How about you go clean up, and we'll resume therapy tomorrow after I call Travis."

"Fair enough."

* * *

The next day, Jack and I paid a visit to the Bailey place, along with Dave Dawson, a semi-retired handyman who had once built houses in the area and who had been a member at Riverside Free Will since the first week Ronnie and Sarah started it in a barn on their property. There was still plenty of work to do. A blue tarp covered a third of Travis' roof, which had been severely damaged by the flying steeple that had killed his granddaughter, Imani. Debris from the destroyed mobile homes was still in piles waiting to be hauled off. The little family church needed plenty of repairs, not to mention a new steeple. That's the project the Riverside Men decided they would tackle first, pissing me off. I told Dave that I would pay for all of the repairs to Travis' home if he would make a list of materials needed. Jack agreed with me that Travis' home should be our top priority, so he and JD decided that they would work alongside me instead of the men's group. I was certain they were doing it not so much out of a sense of charity with Travis in mind but more as a desperate attempt to point me in a positive direction for a change.

For much of that Saturday, I was buoyed by actually doing something besides sitting on my ass and drinking my pain away. I was hardly a gifted carpenter, but I had quality tools and had renovated Riley's apartment myself. I wasn't fast, but I'd gotten skilled at pulling out poorly driven nails, re-cutting mismeasured boards and basically doing most steps at least twice. JD had worked with Dave the previous summer and was the de facto foreman of our little crew. Jack was mostly relegated to handing us tools and materials, which was the extent of his construction skills. Travis kept us supplied with water and had the most important job of the day—going to Montezuma to grab a bagful of burgers from Sam's Snack Shack. We stopped for lunch when Travis returned with the grease-soaked bag and a few bottles of Diet Coke.

"Praise Jesus!" I said as we stopped for lunch. "Thanks, Travis."

"I got Diet Cokes—hope that's OK," he said.

"Of course," I said. "It totally offsets the fat and cholesterol."

"Exactly," Travis agreed.

"Can't argue with science," I declared. "These young kids don't understand."

Jack rolled his eyes as he grabbed four burgers and a couple of drinks before heading to the tailgate of my truck to eat with JD. Travis sat on the front porch steps of his home.

"Mind if I join you?" I asked. He motioned his hand as an invitation. He seemed uncomfortable with us white folks crawling all over his house, but he needed the help. "How you holding up?" I asked.

"Not good," he admitted. "I cry every night when I think it's time to tuck..." His voice trailed off, and he looked away to hide his glistening eyes. I wanted to tell him that I could relate. But my daughter was still alive, unlike little Imani. I might have been tortured by my own loss, but I knew it didn't compare to the finality of his.

"I'm so sorry, man. I can't imagine."

"In *His* lovin' arms now," he said as he gazed skyward.

"Yep," I agreed as I also looked up. I knew Imani was not in *his* arms, but if it made Travis feel better, so be it. I envied his having faith to lean upon because I desperately needed something to prop me up besides liquor. If only I could have tricked myself into believing the ridiculous, I might have had some peace. I don't know what happens to us when we're gone. Perhaps there is a soul, some kind of energy that cannot be destroyed and takes a form no human can yet understand. Or maybe we're just worm food. The possibility of having a soul floating into a mysterious new existence is one of the last things I clung to as my justification for remaining a church goer as a youth, just in case that existence involved a guy taking roll outside some pearly gates. But even that motivation faded when I reasoned that the imaginary sky dwellers would never let *me* decide what happened to my soul anyway, so what was the point of worrying about it while I was alive? I was about fifteen when I made the call to quit worrying about my soul altogether. I delegated that responsibility to my extended family, unbeknownst to them. With no soul to worry about, I had no use for any of man's religions.

The conversation shifted to the safe space of my asking, "Whatever happened to...?" about various old schoolmates. I couldn't remember the last time I opened Facebook, which is where I probably could have found most of them if I truly wanted to. I had gotten weary of seeing all the fake versions of people's perfect lives on social media while my all too real life was going to hell.

"I reckon you did about as good as anybody from our class," Travis said between chomps of his double-cheeseburger.

"Weren't you working on Wall Street or living in New York or something?"

"Yep, on both counts. Hated it after a while, though."

"And didn't you marry a sister?"

"My sister? Hell, I don't even really like her. Besides, this ain't Alabama."

"No, *a sista*."

"Yeah, I'm kidding. She hated it here. So did my daughter."

"Why didn't y'all just go back to New York?" he asked.

"Because I thought they would someday see what I saw in Possum Holler. I guess the joke's on me because, unfortunately, I'm starting to see what *they* saw in Possum Holler."

"Go somewhere else. I know you got the money."

"I probably should...someday. I just always felt like this was supposed to be home."

"I know what you mean," Travis said with the closest thing to a smile that I'd witnessed from him. "Look around, man. This is all *family* land. Couldn't leave if I wanted to. You oughta sail off to the Caribbean or something. And send me a postcard since I ain't going no damn where."

"Well, there's no point in me leaving Possum Holler until I've worked on myself. Wherever you go, there you are. *There* always sounds like a better place, but when you get *there*, here you are. *There* becomes *here*. It should be, 'wherever you go, here you are.' Know what I mean?"

"You on drugs? You sound like Mucho Loco!"

"Wow, now *there's* somebody I haven't thought about in a long time!" I said. "Whatever happened to him anyway?"

"Believe it or not, he's still around."

Daniel Hernandez was a senior when we were freshmen in high school and was far better known as Mucho Loco. I'm not sure whether he got the nickname for being crazy or because he was as big as a locomotive. He was 6-foot-7 and over 400 pounds. He played offensive tackle in high school and scared the shit out of opponents when our team first walked onto the field, especially the 190-pound defensive linemen who realized they would have to line up opposite him. After kickoff, though, they realized why he was not a major college football prospect: He may have been as big as a locomotive, but he was slower than a derailed train. They simply outran him to the backfield and blew up every play. No wonder our team went 1-9 his senior year—and that win came by forfeit.

Mucho Loco's after-school "job" was selling marijuana out of a purple '77 Oldsmobile Delta 88, a car as gargantuan as he was and commonly known by his young customers as "The Batmobile." He was not a scary drug dealer. He was a gentle fellow, always smiling and never pushing hard drugs. Then again, he might have always been smiling because he accepted multiple forms of payment from the area's skankier girls.

"I'm kinda surprised he's still alive," I said. "I figured he would have died of a heart attack or bled to death getting a blowjob from a snaggletoothed girl."

"Shoot, I bet you weigh more than he does," Travis said with a chuckle.

"Maybe after these Samburgers."

"Naw, man, I'm serious. Mucho Loco lost mucho *fat*," he insisted. "You know, he used to drive the tour bus for some Southern rock white boy band named Flamin' Haybales or some redneck shit like that. I think he also kept 'em high. But he got a bad back, and doctors told him if he didn't lose weight, he wouldn't be able to walk much longer."

"Damn."

"Well, one of them band fellas took him on a trip to one of them retreats in South America—Peru, I think—some of that Aaron Rodgers shit, and he came back a changed man. Lost like 200 pounds. He's skinny as hell now. Looks like a big ass white pencil."

"Seriously? Where's he at now?"

"Same place a few miles north of Oglethorpe. He never actually left—he just was hardly ever home. Lived on the road. But his folks left him all that land off Whitewater Creek, same place he used to grow weed."

"Used to?"

"Yeah, he's all into growing mushrooms and weird herbs and shit. He got disability because of his back and doesn't work. He just grows veggies and herbs and does art. Oh, he also rents out some little cabins and has some kind of meditation or yoga thing."

"Interesting," I said. "You been there?"

"Only mushrooms I do are on pizza," he said. "I haven't been out there since we were in school. I see him every now and then at that little farmer's market they do some Saturdays in downtown Oglethorpe. He usually has a little booth with 'maters and stuff. Good'uns, too."

"You know, in the ten years I've been back in Possum Holler, I've never once gone to that farmer's market," I said. "Maybe I'll check it out next weekend. Downtown huh?"

"Yeah, all one block of it."

We finished off the little burgers and small talk, then went back to work. I let the teenagers JD and Jack climb the ladder back to the roof where they were patching one of several holes above Imani's bedroom. None of the Christians around me who were working so hard to help the also very Christian Bailey family saw a speck of symbolism in her tragic death. If God were on trial for manslaughter, the tattered pieces of that steeple would have been entered as evidence.

"Uncle Ben, toss me that nail gun while you ain't doing nothin'!" JD yelled from above as I stood alongside a couple of rickety wooden sawhorses that one of the Riverside Free Will guys had crafted many years ago. The roof was low, so it wasn't a difficult toss, even with a heavy nail gun connected by a hose to the air compressor. So, I thought little of it. I wish I had.

The nail gun sailed within a few inches of JD's outstretched hands before it fell back toward me. I tried to catch it, but it slammed my left hand's middle finger between it and the sawhorse. Actually, the nail gun didn't so much *fall* my way. It violently snapped back toward me because my dumb ass didn't know I was standing on the hose.

"Goddammit!" I yelled as I tried to shake off the pain.

When folks yell that on a job site, it garners pretty quick attention, though accidents are common when there's a mix of skilled and unskilled volunteers. But it gets extra attention when you holler it on a job site with a couple dozen church-going volunteers. The din of saws and hammering paused, and several guys ran my way, likely fearing I'd sawed off something valuable based upon my flailing.

"What happened?" a breathless Larry Pickett asked on the run ahead of the others who were less concerned judging by their normal-speed walks.

"Arghh," I said. "Nothing, nothing—I just smashed my driving finger trying to catch a nail gun. I'll be fine. It just hurts like a mutha—like, real bad."

"What do you mean 'driving finger?'" Jack asked as he and JD landed back on terra firma. "Is that a golf thing?"

"No," JD explained. "That's how he communicates with other drivers."

"What can you communicate with a finger?" Jack said, prompting a clarification from me.

"With *this* finger, a lot, such as: Did your car come with a blinker? What does the word *yield* mean on your planet? Perhaps ten inches is not a safe following distance. Nice bumper sticker, you racist redneck! I don't know if I can drive without it."

I liked Larry because he was more of a Jesus-y Christian than most of the folks at Riverside Free Will who were more worried about "woke" issues "destroying" America. He was more into actions of quiet faith than evangelizing. He was the only person I knew from our area who once attended annual protests outside Fort Benning's School of the Americas (later the Western Hemisphere Institute for Security Cooperation) in Columbus. He would stand outside the gates and join the vigils, but he never got arrested nor crossed the line as many did, especially in the '90s and early 2000s. I respected his tempered dissent. Still, I was uncomfortable when he took my hand. Then he instructed everyone to bow their heads for a moment.

"Dear Lord, we ask for your healing hands—and your mercifulness—for brother Ben as he has joined your flock in this righteous calling, to be your hands and feet, sharing love in this world. In your name we pray. Amen."

During the quick prayer, I looked around to see who was peeking. All the Riverside guys did indeed close their eyes, though Stan Harris nodded and smirked when Larry asked for mercy, apparently compiling a mental list of the things I needed mercy for. Jack had one eye open, and when I caught it, he just shrugged his shoulders as if to say, "Hey, couldn't hurt." As they returned to their posts, I patted Larry on the back.

"Appreciate that, Larry, but it's just a finger."

"Hey, I've seen many faith healings," he said. "I once saw a broken leg healed during a mission trip in Honduras and saw a deaf boy hear again after the pastor stuck his fingers in his ears three times."

"I guess if he stuck them in there four times, well, that'd just be crazy," I said.

"The Lord's got this—you just gotta have a little faith."

"Yeah, I always thought the Falcons might have won a couple of Super Bowls with Benny Hinn as head trainer."

Larry chuckled and walked away, confident that I was in good hands. He clearly didn't know me as well as some of the others. If there was a big guy upstairs keeping score on everybody, he damn sure wasn't about to heal my finger anytime soon.

"Guess that means I'm screwed, huh?" I muttered to JD and Jack.

"Well, your finger might be," JD said.

"You might need to head to the hospital," Jack chimed in.

"What country do you think this is?" I asked. "You want me to lose everything? I'd get a bill from the doctor, the X-ray technician, the radiologist who looks at the X-ray, the radiology assistant who sniffs the X-ray, the nurse who waves hello, and then I'd get a note from the insurance company denying my claim with the heading 'Nice try.' No thank you. I'll blow on it or something and take some ibuprofen when I get home. Maybe soak it in a frozen margarita. You know, those have magic healing powers, too."

The boys' exasperated looks told me I'd gone on long enough.

"Get back to work," I said. "Maybe carry the nail gun with you this time. If there's really something wrong with my finger, I'll get it seen about. I've jammed it a million times. I'm sure it's no big deal."

"Yeah," JD said. "I can tell by the way it's swelling up and turning colors that it's probably just jammed. Geez, Uncle Ben, it's not the first time I've seen this. It's broke."

"And if I go to the hospital, *I'll* be broke. Now get back to work and let's get all this do-goodin' done."

# Mucho Loco

In case you're wondering, soaking in a frozen margarita does *not* heal a broken finger—though I certainly gave it a shot, literally and figuratively. Neither does praying. So, I broke down, so to speak, and took my smashed finger to the urgent care clinic down the road in Americus. They put it in a splint that I was ordered to wear for four weeks. On the bright side, that made my driving finger even more expressive:

"WHAT DOES THE WORD *YIELD* MEAN ON YOUR PLANET?"

I guess there are *some* advantages to this broken son of a bitch, I thought, though I didn't need my finger's new all-caps voice to speak much over the following week as I left the house only a couple of times to get basic necessities, such as liquor, mixers, and food. Normally content to sit around my house and pool on weekends after a school week or during normal summer breaks, I was getting bored and restless as an officially unemployed person. Usually when that happened, I would grab my acoustic guitar and perform a few songs for the squirrels. I've never told anyone this before, but Jimmy Buffett taught me how to play guitar. Actually, even he doesn't—well, *didn't* know that. In the 1990s, I began developing my below-average guitar skills by strumming along to my favorite Buffett tunes through the years —first with chordbooks and later with chords printed from the internet or scrolling tablature and chord apps on my phone. I still consider myself more of a guitar *owner* than a guitar player. I do know a ton of chords, but the fingers of my right hand just aren't nimble enough to pluck the strings correctly. So, I'm just a plain ol' boring strummer. However, I could not play *any* chords with a broken finger. No squirrels complained about my concert postponements, not that you can trust those nuts.

JD shepherded Jack around the area all week long to help with the sociology project. Jack came home each afternoon with a contented smile, seemingly energized to retreat into his apartment and make sense of his notes. I didn't know whether he looked happy because he was gleaning useful perspectives on Southern living or because he was actually an undercover agent finding comedy gold for writers in Hollywood—or "Y'allywood" around Atlanta, which has about as many Yankees as Hollywood. No matter what put that smile on his face, it annoyed me to see someone so easily placated while I was so irritable.

On Saturday morning, I made the radical decision to leave the house and engage with the outside world. I woke up early, for me anyway. I rolled out of bed at 8:45, indulged in a hot shower, and was out the door by 9:30. Travis had planted a seed in my head about this little farmer's market in "downtown" Oglethorpe. I'm not sure why I'd never checked it out before, but it likely had something to do with the fact that it was over by noon. I wasn't a morning person. Even in New York, I resented the fact that folks kept to conformist schedules. Hell, even the Stock Exchange waited until 9:30 a.m. to wake up.

When I was growing up, Oglethorpe had about 1,000 residents and one traffic light. By the time I returned from New York, the population had plummeted to about 900 residents, but the town remained steady at one traffic light. Amazingly enough, in the mid-1800s, this town was one of Georgia's most thriving cities with about 20,000 inhabitants. It was the terminus of a major railroad line at that point and boasted fancy hotels with orchestras that entertained the guests. It was about as gilded a city as the state could muster outside of Savannah and Atlanta. In fact, it was once even considered for Georgia's state capital, but malaria and smallpox ravaged Oglethorpe and turned it into a near ghost town by the end of the 19th century. Though some buildings were burned to the ground and others torn down, there were a few remnants of the glory days downtown. It was along the sidewalks in front of these monuments to the past that the farmer's market was staged.

"Ben Peachy?!"

Sandra Griffin's voice was unmistakable and quintessentially Southern. When I was young, she was the receptionist for Dr. Chapman, the only family practitioner in town. She was a tall, classy lady whose voice dripped with so much honey that hundreds of folks got diabetes just from talking to her. She was appealing to the eyes, no doubt, but it was that voice that drove every man in town wild, even though they all had grown up around plenty of other women with Southern accents. They would call the doctor's office just to hear her answer. Her husband was a giant of a man, a successful farmer, and a really decent guy. He was quiet, calm, and religious. Our families attended the same church, and I looked up to him. Well, I looked up to him until 1986 when he got wind of a couple of guys who were calling up Mrs. Sandra nearly every day. That's when he calmly walked into Rack-em-Up, a pool hall/bar just outside of town and proceeded to beat the ever-loving shit out of both of them. After that, he terrified me.

Mrs. Sandra quit the doctor's office shortly thereafter and opened a hair salon in "downtown" Oglethorpe. My mother had cut my hair in a horrible bowl style until that point. Then they began paying Mrs. Sandra a whopping ten bucks to handle it, thank goodness. Over the next several years, I wound up hearing that sweet, unintentionally sultry voice more than any of those harassers because cutting my hair took over a half-hour. It's not that I had a complicated style. It's just that Mrs. Sandra's greatest —and perhaps only—sin was that she gossiped. Unlike most stylists, though, she could not gossip *and* cut hair at the same time. She would flail her scissors around as she spoke. I was grateful to flee the salon with both of my eyeballs unpunctured, often saying "whew, still alive" after the door closed behind me.

Despite the dangerous conditions, I recalled only one bad haircut I ever got there, and it was after her daughter Jessica came home with a hickey after we hung out one night at my house while my parents were in Memphis, where my dad had business and where my mom toured Graceland. I toured Jessica a bit that night but never made it to her Jungle Room. I like to believe the one bad haircut coming within a week of the hickey was purely coincidental. Sugary-sweet Southern belles are only vengeful in books and movies. Although, she would make a great character in the novel I still suspected Jack might be writing under the guise of research.

"Hey, Mrs. Sandra, how are you?" I tried to give her a quick, polite hug, but she pulled me in tighter. I knew at least a dozen men who would give their monthly Social Security checks to be where I was at that moment, so I savored it in their honor. She was no Jennifer Jacobs from tennis camp, but she wasn't bad for a senior citizen.

"Why, I ain't seen you in at least ten years," she said with the familiar drawl that any respected Hollywood director would decry as over the top and unrealistic. "What brings you downtown? You need a haircut, darlin'?"

"Which one?" It was a joke about my thinning hair, but she didn't get it.

"Whichever one you want, honey."

"Actually, I'm just down here to get some 'maters and stuff. Never been here for this thing. Pretty crowded." I was referring to the three dozen folks browsing upwards of eight tables and booths.

"You should have been here about eight o'clock," she said. "It was packed! Well, except for that tall fella's booth down there. You remember Daniel?" she said, glancing toward the tall man about forty yards up the sidewalk as I nodded in the affirmative. "He just got here about an hour ago. He's a little weird." Then she whispered with her hand politely shielding her gossiping mouth, "I think he might be on drugs."

"Well, this *is* America," I noted. "We're *all* on drugs now. Good seeing you, Ms. Sandra."

Thanks to Travis, I knew the tall fella was Mucho Loco. Had he not tipped me off that he had lost a crazy amount of weight, I'd have never recognized him. He sported long gray hair in a ponytail and a beard fit for a skinny Santa Claus. With his tie-dyed shirt, he reminded me of the great basketball star and renowned deadhead Bill Walton. No one was at his small folding table, where he was making sure his small stack of rack cards was neat and orderly. Small baskets of tomatoes, peaches, blueberries and onions lined the table. He also had some tiny clear plastic containers with what appeared to be mushrooms.

"Mucho Loco!"

"Hey! Actually, it's Daniel. And you're?"

"Ben Peachy. I was a few years behind you in school."

"Peachy? I knew some Peachys back in the day. Did you have a sister?"

"Still do, not that she'd claim me," I said. "Sarah."

"Ahh, I *do* remember. She used to—"

"Well, enough reminiscing about her," I interrupted, not wanting to know where *that* conversation was going. "I remember seeing you play football and—"

"Well, enough reminiscing about those days," he interrupted, apparently not wanting any analysis of his high school football underperformances.

"Fair enough. What's this?" I asked as I picked up one of the rack cards topped by the words *Querencia Valley*.

"A few cabins I rent out. Also got a yoga studio, sweat lodge, greenhouses, gardens. Even hosted a few intimate weddings. Mainly old friends from the Atlanta area."

"Interesting," I said as I kept reading. I could feel him watching me—from high above.

"You serious?" he asked.

"Yeah." I looked up and nodded to confirm that I was not bullshitting him.

"Sorry, brother. This is not the kind of thing folks around here are usually into. They think I'm out there devil worshiping or something."

"You some kind of warlock?" I asked with a smile.

"*Well*...just kidding. Of course, if you don't go to church around here, look like a Deadhead and spend a lot of time alone, you might as well be a warlock. Right?"

"I know exactly what you mean—except I'm a Parrot Head," I said. "I don't guess you ever got to drive a bus for the Grateful Dead or Jimmy Buffett, did you?"

"No, the biggest acts I ever drove for were Dr. Hook and The Little River Band. Drove all over the U.S.—Australia, too. Mostly just regional bands across the Southeast. What'd you say your name was again? I'm sorry. Brain fog."

"Ben. Ben Peachy."

"Why don't you come out and see the place? I've actually got a handful of folks coming over tonight for a pick 'n' grin—a couple of them from a band I used to drive for. You play?"

"Guitar? Well, I'm a guitar *owner* and a strummer at best. Some Sunday afternoons—well, until recently anyway—I'd do a little pickin' and grinnin' on the back porch with my nephew, Sarah's son. Taught him everything I know—poor kid."

"Well, come on out and hang with us peace-loving warlocks and freaks. They're some of the best musicians who've never made it big—well, not too big anyway. A couple of 'em you might've heard of."

"Can you summon the ghost of Jimi Hendrix?"

"That's a tall order," he said while I waited for a "no pun intended" that never came. "Would you settle for the ghost of Jim Croce?"

"You know, he was an underrated player," I said.

"Indeed," Daniel said. "Think you can strum along to *Operator*?"

"No, but I do a kick-ass version of *Twinkle Twinkle Little Star*. Well, I *did*. See this smashed finger? Can't play a damn chord right now. It'll be a few weeks, I'm afraid."

"Well, then just come on out and chill out with us. We'll have a bonfire, and you can just hang out. It'd actually be kinda nice to have a local out there for a change. My friends think I'm the only person who lives around here."

"Is it BYOB?" I asked.

"No alcohol," he insisted. "Gave that up years ago. Don't smoke anything, either, or take any pills. In fact, I have a friend coming down to stay the weekend who goes to a temple where they are allowed to use ayahuasca—for religious purposes, of course."

"*Aya-what-a*?"

"Ayahuasca. You make tea with it, and my friend leads the ceremony. It's a South American thing, but there are a few spots in the U.S. where it's legal—or *kinda* legal—including a temple in Atlanta. Trust me—it's a mind-expanding experience unlike anything you could imagine."

"I don't know," I said. "My mind's pretty freakin' huge already. Only got so much room in the ol' skull for expansion."

"It affects everyone differently," he said, turning serious. "But let me tell you what I get out of it every single time. I *see* peace. I *feel* it...for *weeks* afterward. It changed my life. If everyone had just a tiny sample of that peace, the world would be a very different place, a better place."

*Peace*—now that was something I hadn't experienced in the years since Elizabeth fled Georgia, followed shortly thereafter by Riley. I was intrigued. Mucho—er, I mean, Daniel certainly seemed healthy and content even while looking different from anyone who lived within twenty miles of Possum Holler. Heck, compared to him, *I* was a conformist. He stuck out like a sore thumb—or like a sore middle finger, or like a 6-foot-7 skinny bearded guy in a tie-dyed shirt in the middle of bustling downtown Oglethorpe, Georgia and its one traffic light.

"You know what? I'm game. What time?"

"Be there at four o'clock, and you can join us for an early dinner," he said. "You might want to skip lunch—need to save plenty of room. Then, we'll have a little pick 'n' grin before the ceremony."

"Can I bring something? What ya having?"

"The guys have requested my specialty—a giant pot of vegetarian chili," he proudly proclaimed.

"Cool," I said, faking interest in chili without meat. "Can't wait." I was most definitely going to have a sandwich or a couple of Samburgers for lunch.

"Address is on that card," he said. "Just look for the metal *QV* sign a couple miles north of Whitewater off 128. It's about a quarter-mile down a gravel road. You've got to drive past my cabins and just keep going until you see my place."

"I assume your place is easy to spot," I said.

"I promise you—there is *no way* you can miss it. It's colorful and very, um, *different*. And it's at the end of the road, the very end. You'll see."

"OK, *that* doesn't sound scary at all," I said with an abundance of sarcasm. "But if I see a bunch of warlocks flying around on brooms, I'm turning around."

"Fair enough!" he said with a laugh and a gentle slap on the back. "If I see that, I'm doing the same! I ain't crazy!"

"You sure?"

"Well, maybe *un poco loco. Mucho, no mas.*"

* * *

When I got back to the house, I was surprised to see JD and Jack packing camping supplies into the bed of JD's rolling Tractor Supply already full of tools and farm supplies.

"You can't leave Possum Holler, boy!" I yelled as I slammed the door to my truck in faux outrage. "You ain't leaving me alone here in paradise."

"We're leaving you to your kingdom tonight," JD said. "Going camping."

"And fishing," Jack chimed in.

"*We*? Jack, you realize we don't camp in hotels down here. And we don't do our fishing at Captain D's."

"We're going to Whitewater Park and do a little tent camping," JD explained. "And, tonight, we're gonna be frying up a mess of crappie."

"That's crappie with an *ie* not a *y*, Jack," I clarified.

"I'll have you know I'm quite the angler," Jack said.

"Scooping up goldfish at PetSmart doesn't count," I retorted.

"Trust me," he said with a grin, "if I can handle a twenty-pound striper in Massachusetts, I think I can pull in a one-pound bluegill in Georgia."

"Well, excuse me, Captain Ahab." I sensed they might have some concern that I would invite myself along. I'd had enough of sleeping in a hot, humid tent during our little Florida adventure and didn't have any interest in being their wobbly third wheel, so I put their minds at ease.

"Well, y'all have fun. I'm actually headed to a pick 'n' grin with some friends tonight—not far from Whitewater actually."

"You can't—" JD started.

"Have friends? As implausible as it seems—"

"No," he corrected. "You can't play with that finger of yours."

"Well, even if my finger was OK, for me it'd just be a strum 'n' grin for me," I said. "I guess tonight will just be a grin 'n' grin."

"You know how to grin?" Jack asked, feigning disbelief.

"Check this out," I said as I gave them a pained half-smile.

"You're scaring us," JD said. "Don't do that right before we go camping in the dark."

"That's the most frightening thing I've seen since I left Boston," Jack said.

"Seriously," JD agreed. "Scariest thing I've *ever* seen."

"Watch for gators," I warned them. "I hear there's a couple at Whitewater that have a taste for smart-ass."

* * *

I didn't make a margarita that afternoon, nor did I take a gummy. I took a nap instead and forgot to eat lunch. Whatever this experience was going to be, I wanted to be *present* for it. I was intrigued, and I needed something to fill the gaps in my life. I was no believer in organized—or even *disorganized*—religion, and I had just about as many doubts about these ayahuasca experiences everyone from Aaron Rodgers to Daniel was touting. I did a little googling, and just about everyone who truly immersed themselves in the ayahuasca ceremonies said it changed them for the better. Of course, I knew plenty of folks who had found Jesus through the years and had similar reviews. I suspected a significant level of bullshit was part of both experiences, and a few more online searches confirmed that a shot of ayahuasca might even *taste* like bullshit—or dirt or burnt coffee or bitter chocolate or prune juice depending upon the reviewer. Oh, and as a lovely side effect, a lot of folks vomit. Between vegetarian chili and whatever prune dirt bullshit juice this ayahuasca was, I knew there was a damn good chance that I was going to be in the "lot of folks" category, a place I rarely found myself, and I'd seen enough Big Pharma commercials that I didn't want to know the litany of side effects in advance. I prefer to be surprised by things like explosive diarrhea and an itchy perineum.

# Demons & Angels

I put the address for Querencia Valley into my Google Maps and headed north out of Possum Holler. It may very well be the first and only time in my life that I needed satellite assistance to find anything in Macon County. Until then, it was more of a "turn down yonder way just past where Crazy Jimmy crashed his truck into that giant oak tree that ain't there no more" kind of place. I doubted anyone with one of those Google camera-topped vehicles had ever traversed Pine Level Road toward Querencia Valley, yet, sure enough, there was a Google image with a simple *QV* sign just a few miles north of Whitewater Creek Park. Hell, even I hadn't seen that sign before. More power to ya, Google! With that oak tree gone after Crazy Jimmy's tragic incident, I might have never found it without technological assistance.

Although the sign was simple, the colors were not—a bright blue *Q* and an orange *V*, underneath which were the words Querencia Valley spelled out in a military-style stencil. Nothing blended. Perhaps that was the point. The gravel road wound through thin pine trees that looked to have been planted about ten years earlier in neat rows, though they needed thinning if they were to be worthy of harvesting in another decade or so. Then again, Mucho Loco, er, I mean Daniel may not have shared his parents' interest in tree harvesting. He apparently had less typical interests for our neck of the woods. That intrigued me.

After the third bend in the road, the pines stopped on the right side at an opening with a pond encircled by six tiny wooden cabins. They looked like the old sharecropper homes that dotted the landscapes around Possum Holler, except these weren't falling down under the combined weight of time and kudzu. I figured these were the VRBOs to which Travis had referred. A couple of cabins had cars parked alongside them. I could see why some folks from overcrowded cities might want to rent them, but they were a little too close to each other for my liking. If it were just one cabin with that front porch overlooking the pond, I could live in it just fine by myself. But the thought of having next-door neighbors, even temporary ones, gave me the heebie-jeebies—but not as much as what I saw next.

The gravel road ended at two concrete totems, each about ten feet tall and adorned with shapes and designs in multiple colors. Yellow and orange flames passed for their hair. One face bore a cheesy smile, while the other was in the midst of a full-on Munch-ish *Scream*. The opening between the totems was just wide enough for my truck with about a foot to spare on each side. I drove slowly and carefully between them, wondering if this might be the last time I drove anywhere.

Extending from each totem was a concrete wall that hemmed in Daniel's home. The outside of the barrier was a dull gray, but the inside was decorated with colorful spirals, circles, waves, suns, stars, moons, and more faces, though each of these visages seemed either peaceful or downright asleep. Smaller totems dotted the area, along with random wooden bridges over nothing in particular. There were smaller structures, each of which had every square inch painted in loud colors and shapes with the exception of a large but otherwise ordinary greenhouse. Years ago, that greenhouse likely contained marijuana plants, but these days it likely was home to mushrooms and herbs, some of which might have even been possibly sorta legal.

At the center of it all was the house—a typical small farmhouse with a front porch swing and craftsman-style features. It's where Daniel grew up, although I suspect back then the exterior walls were simple and white. Not anymore. Each of the four exterior sides was painted a different color—flaming yellow, dark blue, soft orange, and bright pink. I didn't know of another house in the area with any *one* of those exterior colors, and I was a thousand percent sure there was no other house within a hundred miles painted in all four such colors. Daniel's tucked-away world was an explosion of color and weirdness. It looked as though a Grateful Dead concert's T-shirt stand had exploded there.

I parked on a concrete pad in front of the house where three other vehicles were parked. A beautifully restored cherry red '50s-era Chevy 3100 pickup was the only one bearing a local license plate from Macon County. The other two cars—a gray Nissan Sentra and a white Honda Civic—each had Fulton County plates. I suspected they were rentals.

The familiar bang of a screen door snapping back to its frame shattered the quiet, followed by the bellowing voice of the quirky giant.

"You made it!" he yelled gleefully. "No warlocks?"

"You sound surprised," I said.

"No, I've never actually seen a warlock—well, except for a couple on the trail cam."

"I mean you sound surprised that I made it," I corrected.

"For good reason," Daniel said as he reached the bottom of the stairs while I extended my hand for a shake only to be ensnared in a bear hug—well, more like a Bigfoot-hug. "I bet I haven't had a local person visit here in at least five years."

"Seriously?" I asked. "Who was the last?"

"The tax assessor, Mr. Mullis."

"I thought Mr. Mullis died," I said with a hint of concern that Daniel no doubt picked up on.

"He did." He left space for a dramatic pause, then laughed. "Heart attack."

"Must've hit him when he saw this place."

Daniel chuckled. "He was a little taken aback when he visited, yes, but he actually had a heart attack while cheating on his wife a couple years later...with one of my relatives, no less."

"Damn. Your Aunt Carol?" I asked pryingly.

"No, Uncle Larry. And don't besmirch my sweet Aunt Carol's name."

"So, what's the story with this, um, colorful place? I'm not judging, mind you. It's just different. You know folks don't do *different* around here."

"Don't I know it! I'm sort of an amateur folk artist, and, well, I like color."

"That's not so weird," I said with a relieved smile.

"And the faces are spirits I've met through the years."

"That, on the other hand, *is* weird," I responded, prompting a hearty laugh from Daniel, who slapped me on the back again.

"Normal's boring," he said as we walked around the side of the house.

"I know a thing or two about boring," I admitted as I looked upon the green spaces and gardens to the side and back of the home. "Wow, these grounds are mighty lush."

"You've got to *talk* to the plants—that's the secret ingredient," he said matter-of-factly, or so I thought. "I'm kidding. It's rained a good bit lately. That's the *actual* secret ingredient."

"Well, who'd've thunk it? Of course, your pine trees back yonder are growing so well, they might need a little thinning."

"When it comes to trees, I'm a grower, not a sower. Actually, my father planted those right before he died. I don't know if he planned to harvest them or not, but I like that they shield Querencia from the so-called *real world*," he said while making air quotes with his fingers.

When we got to the back of the house, I saw several guys sitting on benches within another concrete wall, this one octagonal and about three feet high. Again, it was painted in bright colors with a multitude of faces, eyes and shapes. In the middle of the octagon was a massive metal fire pit with wood arranged for a fire that I figured would play a major role in the night ahead. We walked through a gap in the wall and approached the men.

"Hey, fellas. This is my friend Ben. He's actually a local boy like me. And different, also like me."

"Not *that* different," I said with a smile as I extended my hand toward the men who walked my way. They were comfortably dressed in shorts and t-shirts, but none of them dressed like Deadheads. Instead of shaking my hand, though, they each hugged me one by one, vigorously. I appreciated the intention but not the touchy-feely-ness.

"Most of these guys I met during my bus driver days," he said as he began introducing them one by one. "That's Dave, Jimmy, Stan, Jorge, Lucas and Hank." Lucas and Hank each wielded an acoustic guitar.

"I guess y'all are doing the pickin' and we're doing the grinnin'," I said to Lucas and Hank as Daniel retreated into the house.

"We'll pass 'em around," said Lucas, who wore his light brown hair in a short ponytail, while the others sported haircuts much less like Daniel and Lucas and a lot more like models for a Great Clips poster. "You play?" he asked.

"I'm a guitar *owner*," I explained. "I strum a little. Well, I *did* until I smashed this finger anyway."

"Damn, bro," he said. "You flip somebody off too hard?"

"Was helping a friend with some tornado recovery work—not very well, as you can see."

"Y'all come on in," Daniel interrupted as he held open a screen door that led to his back porch and a couple of long picnic tables. "Chili's ready!"

The screened-in back porch was perfectly normal for an old country home. It lacked the color of the exterior and grounds, but it was classic. I had been a conformist for most of my pre-shit-hitting-the-fan life, and I felt far more at home on that porch than in the ring of color and crazy faces staring at me. I was more than a little worried that these faces might be hopping out of the walls when we finally got around to the ayahuasca festivities. However, this early dinner seemed utterly normal, like a gathering of guys who *looked* like a bunch of good ol' country boys but probably *voted* like a bunch of good ol' city boys. I was comfortable and felt welcomed for a change.

The guys shared inside stories of life on the road—drinking, drugs, women, encounters with cops who mistook them for riff-raff, and such. If I knew how to write, I could have penned a whole novel from what I heard at that dinner. Most were my age or slightly older, except for Lucas, the ponytailed fellow who'd asked if I played. While most of the guys rarely still performed, if at all, it was clear that Lucas was present-day road warrior.

"I take it you're still on the road?" I queried the young man directly across from me.

"On a little hiatus right now," he said with a sigh. "Lately, I've been hopping on stage when folks like Drivin N Cryin, Marshall Tucker Band, the Outlaws, and such play around Atlanta."

"I think Kevin Kinney of Drivin N Cryin might be one of the most underrated artists of all-time," I blurted out.

"Yeah," Lucas confirmed. "Great guy, too. Definitely still got it."

"So, are you rock, country or what?"

"That's kind of the problem—or, the problem with the industry anyway," he said. "I don't fit into any category, but, at the same time, I don't want to fit in. I'm OK with flying under the radar a little bit."

"I can definitely respect that," I said.

"I just can't put my music in a sellable box, man, and they don't like that. They don't understand that I don't *need* to be a superstar, not that I would be. I like being able to walk down streets without being recognized. Even back home in the mountains, I'm just Lucas Parsons, the best punter Elbert County football ever had!"

"Lucas Parsons," I repeated as I scratched my head. "Why does that name sound so familiar? I'm not exactly an expert on Elbert County football."

"The handful of folks who do know me probably know me from the Brasstown Baldies," he said.

"That's it! Holy shit!" I yelled.

"You're a fan?"

"I've heard y'all's stuff from my nephew. Good music. He absolutely loves y'all! He's all into non-mainstream music. He tried to explain it by saying y'all were like Joni Mitchell and Lynyrd Skynyrd had a baby."

"I've never thought of it that way," Lucas said while rubbing his stubbly chin. "Although, Lynyrd was a cute fella."

"Um—" I started to explain.

"I'm kiddin', dude," he said as he stood and reached across the table to put his hand on my shoulder as the other guys guffawed. "You gotta lighten up if you're gonna hang with us clowns."

"Man, J.D.'s gonna freak when I tell him about this," I said.

"Your nephew?" he asked.

"Yeah."

"He live around here?"

"Yeah."

"Well, hell, tell him to come on!"

"I don't know if that's fair to Daniel to start dragging more folks he doesn't really know out here."

"The more, the merrier," Daniel insisted. "Seriously. I've spent too much time with these same ol' misfits. Get some young blood out here."

"He's actually fishing and camping over at Whitewater—with a college kid from Boston who's staying in my studio apartment for a few weeks," I explained. "He's working on some kind of sociology project about the South, wants to see it from all angles."

"Then he's *gotta* come," Daniel insisted. "We can't have him going back to Boston thinking everybody down here's some stereotypical redneck chugging PBRs and worshiping the Georgia Bulldogs."

"Hey, PBR is highly underrated!" one of the fellows from the opposite end of the table interjected.

"And what you got against my Bulldogs?" I asked. "Don't tell me you are some sicko Gator or Bama fan!"

"Dude, I don't remember the last time I even *saw* a football game. Not really into it anymore."

I feigned a heart attack, prompting a laugh from the others and a "Go Dawgs!" from one.

"Look," Daniel said as he glared directly at me. "Everybody around this table is a Southerner. Hell, I think almost everybody here is from Georgia. And none of us here—including you, I suspect—is *normal* for around here. Normal people are weird."

"Well, I'm definitely not normal," I said. "Glad to know I'm also not weird."

"Actually, there are a lot more folks in Georgia like you and me than you know. You may not fit in around Possum Holler, but you're not as unique as you think. There are plenty of genuine Southern folks who don't fit the stereotype. They're as Southern as anyone else, but they just don't fit in. So, they fit *out*."

"That doesn't make sense," I said. "How many PBRs have you had?

"Since 1994, none."

"Weird."

"Invite the kids," he said. "It'll be educational. Besides, we've got this superstar here they'd love to meet."

"Who?" Lucas asked with a smile.

"Your dumb ass," a cowboy-looking fellow next to him said.

"Damn, I was hoping I was gonna meet Elvis," Lucas said.

"Depending on how strong this batch is tonight, you still might," his friend said.

* * *

By the time JD and Jack nervously approached the octagon an hour later, orange flames crackled in the fire pit while a couple of the guys, including Lucas, plucked and strummed tunes by Willie Nelson, Steve Earle, and Bob Marley. I could see JD mouth the words "holy shit" when he saw that one of his musical idols was indeed performing in this intimate setting. As Lucas wrapped up the lead vocals of "No Woman, No Cry," I stood up to introduce the boys.

"Fellas, this here's my nephew JD, a big Brasstown Baldies fan, by the way. And this is Jack." I decided to spare him my usual razzing given the unusual setting that even weirded me out before I got lost in the music and the fire. "Jack's from Boston and has come to study us Southerners—and, somehow, we haven't scared him off yet."

"The night's still young," Lucas said as he led the parade of guys to welcome the boys. JD extended his hand, but Lucas playfully slapped it away and gave him a vigorous hug. He then gave Jack a quick half-hug.

"I hear you pick a little," Lucas said as he held his guitar by the neck in front of JD. "It's a pick 'n' grin. How 'bout you pick and I'll grin for a bit?"

"Oh, no, no, no," JD refused. "I'm more of a strummer than a picker. Maybe Jack, though. He's better than I am. Way better. And he can actually sing."

"I'm sorry, what?" I interjected. "I thought you said you sucked."

"I guess it's subjective," Jack said.

"All those times I sat out back and badly strummed Buffett tunes, you didn't say a damn thing."

"You sure he didn't say, 'Please stop'?" JD interjected.

"Can this ayahuasca shit cure smart-assiness?" I asked Daniel.

"I don't know, but for the sake of you boys and every one of these guys over here, I sure hope so!"

"Hey, Jesse!" Lucas shouted to one of the fellas. "You mind if he borrows your strings for a second?"

"No problem," answered Jesse, who looked to be in his late sixties. He wore his long white hair in a ponytail and was dressed in overalls with no shirt. He grunted as he stood up from the wooden bench that Daniel had carved out of a fallen oak tree. His guitar was as weathered as he was with scratches and dozens of signatures upon the face, bearing a striking resemblance to Willie Nelson's Trigger. As he extended it to Jack, I could see many familiar Southern music names such as Dickey Betts, Gary Rossington, Bo Diddley, Jimmie Vaughan, and far more that I didn't recognize but dared not admit in front of those real musicians. "Take care of Ms. Fanny. She's been through it, as you can tell."

"I promise," Jack said. "Why don't you take a load off? And you can put the load right on me." We all stared at Jack—some with mouths agape, including me—as if he had just announced he was from another planet. "You know? The Band? 'The Weight'?"

"Duh!" I blurted out. "How the hell did you know that?"

"Wait!" Lucas interrupted. "So *that's* why you named your guitar Fanny! I'll be damned. That never crossed my mind."

"Well, you're one of them slow North Georgia boys," Jesse said with a smile.

"Aren't you, too?" Lucas asked.

"Hell no!" Jesse responded with faux outrage. "I'm from Hayesville, North Carolina."

"Ah, one of them slow *Carolina* boys," Lucas noted.

"That's better," Jesse said with a chuckle before turning his attention to Jack, who was silently reading the names and examining the instrument. "How 'bout you wow us with something, Stevie Ray?"

"You, too," Lucas insisted while continuing to force his shiny blue guitar upon JD.

"Yeah," I agreed. "Y'all duet us something. Let's Simon and Garfunkel this shit."

"I'm pretty sure duet is not a verb," Jack said.

"And I'm pretty sure y'all are stalling," I argued.

Jack glanced at JD, and they shared a slight nod.

"OK," Jack said. "You mind if we cop a squat on your log there? I can't play standing up. We're not pros like you guys." They sat and began feeling out the strings and frets. "I assume y'all have heard of John Mayer?"

"John who?" Lucas asked.

"He's only one of the best guitarists in America, and if—" Jack said. "You're fucking with me aren't you?"

"Dude, I've got his number in my phone," Lucas responded with a smile. "We could Facetime him if I had my phone with me. Nice guy, but probably busier than I am on Saturday nights."

"Oh yeah, boys." Daniel interrupted. "Be sure to put your phones in the basket on the back porch after this."

JD gave him a thumb's-up and began strumming a light melody reminiscent of "Why Georgia" but more simple than the intricate fingerpicking I'd heard before. Then Jack busted in with the familiar plucking and began to sing. JD kept his head down while focusing on his strumming, but Jack closed his eyes as he sang, never needing to even glance at Ms. Fanny. The professional musicians froze in awe. They *knew* talent. Jack was the closest thing they'd witnessed to somebody being able to nearly match the original version without the notable advantages of having written the song or dating half the nation's Jennifers. I was struck by something else. They played as if *they* had written the song, practiced it, and then made it a staple of their concerts for years. Yet, these boys supposedly had known each other for just a few weeks. I'd been a numbers guy my whole life, and it didn't add up. The other fellas were impressed, while I was stunned but suspicious. I had missed all kinds of signs and red flags in my relationships with Elizabeth and then Riley. What was I missing with these boys?

When they finished, the expert musicians on hand looked around knowingly at each other in silence until Lucas uttered one long Southern drawled, "*Dayummmmmmm.*"

They stood and applauded. You couldn't have scraped the grin off of JD's face with sandpaper as his idol and others came over to slap the boys on the back one by one. It was JD's championship moment, better than the one he nearly experienced on the baseball field. Despite JD's occasional doubts about some of the religious junk that his parents had drilled into his brain through the years, he still believed in God and was certain that God had a plan for him. I knew he was thinking that recent events were all part of a plan to put him in that very spot in that surreal moment in front of his musical idol. It was a high that no cup of ayahuasca could possibly replicate—or so I thought at the time. JD looked to the twilight skies and smiled.

"Jesus Christ," I muttered, knowing that the religious folks had their hooks in him once again. Jack's expression was different. While JD soaked up the appreciation for a performance that he knew was powered mostly by his duet partner's unique talents, Jack looked down sheepishly before glancing my way. I glared at him silently as if he were the proverbial kid caught with his hand in the cookie jar and his fingers wrapped around the last chocolate chip. He knew he was busted. I just wasn't sure what he was busted for.

"Ah, great timing," Daniel said as we all looked up the driveway and saw dust coming from behind a green Subaru Forester that had to be at least twenty years old. At least, I assumed that was dust and not smoke billowing from the rear of the vehicle as it began slowing in front of Daniel's house.

"Who's that?"

"Ana."

"And who's Ana?"

"Our curandero."

"Ahh," I said as I nodded.

"You don't know what that is, do you?" Daniel asked with a smile.

"Well, I have a *colander*-o at the house. I use it to rinse vegetables." Daniel's smile turned into a laugh. "OK, I give. What's a curandero? It ain't like a hooker, is it?"

"You'll see—and you'll thank me later."

"As long as I don't catch anything penicillin can't fix."

“Boys,” Daniel announced, “put your phones in that bucket on the back porch. The ceremony’s about to begin.”

* * *

The last thing I remember from that night at Querencia Valley was the most horrible hallucination that I’ve experienced to this day. Well, I’m eighty percent sure it was my imagination. That leaves a mere twenty percent chance some demons came alive, peeled themselves off of Mucho Loco’s weird wall and dragged me into the nearby woods to torture me with blurry memories and fuzzy premonitions.

The ceremony began with Ana waving around some smoking weeds. She sang a song in Spanish or Incan or something weird and then squatted alongside each fella in the circle and asked them what they were looking for from the night’s experience. I began to suspect they were *all* full of shit, including Ana, but I’d come too far to back out, even after getting a whiff of a cupful of what was allegedly ayahuasca tea. It smelled more like water mixed with moldy dirt from a spot near the creek where Daniel’s dog had been taking shits for the past decade. It tasted far worse, and possessed a texture that went down as smooth as a warm glass of sawdust and sand.

For a while, I felt absolutely nothing. That was hardly shocking. I’d long had a resistance to everything from pot to cold medicine. It often took higher than typical doses for me to get the same responses as others. Maybe I had a tolerance for that awful-tasting ayahuasca mudshake, or perhaps they had me on a mild starter dose, I thought.

Everything then got quiet and still, including me. I'd long before learned how to relax my mind and body to enhance the effects of liquor, gummies, or plain ol' meditation—which, granted, was something I'd shelved in recent years as my personal life spiraled out of my control. I'd abandoned self-improvement for escapism. The more still I became, the more everyone else disappeared. When I felt completely alone, the shadowy face of a girl peeked over the concrete wall and then slowly ducked back behind it. I was certain it was Riley. I steadied myself and walked cautiously to an opening in the octagon. Before going after Riley, I looked back to see if any of the other guys had seen her. They were all gone.

The nightmare then truly began as the strange paintings and sculptures Daniel had created from beings with whom he claimed to have spoken through the years came to life. The sculptures' exteriors cracked and fell away as they took deliberate, zombie-like steps toward me. The colorful creatures painted upon the wall peeled themselves off the concrete and danced toward me like a bunch of demonic Flat Stanleys with evil grins.

Too terrified and woozy to run, I walked briskly from the spooky ceremony space toward the gravel road that I figured Riley must have followed. She definitely wasn't the woodsy type who would detour through the trees. I walked for what seemed like miles and for what I thought was multiple nights. A moment of reality crept into my ayahuasca-altered mind as I remembered the night in Panama City Beach when I had a similar time-bending experience before running into Jenny Jacobs—either for real or in my imagination. I still wasn't sure.

"Riley!" I screamed into the sky as I spun in the middle of the gravel path, desperate to see her again and to decipher my whereabouts. Nothing looked familiar. I was tired of fleeing Daniel's demon buddies and knew Riley was gone, so I sat down to rest.

It was all I could remember as I recounted the night's events to Jack the next morning. I suspected the parts I could not remember were far more terrifying and blocked out.

"Then what?" asked Jack, who was standing with his back to me while gazing out a window.

"Then I woke up in this chair, wherever the hell I am."

"We're in one of Daniel's cabins," he said as he turned to face me.

"How did you find me? I was running all night."

"Dude, you stumbled about fifty feet from Daniel's house and began circling the place. For *hours*."

"No wonder my feet hurt," I said. "Oh God, what about JD? I can't believe I got him into this. I've done messed up again."

"Well, while you were going through hell, he was flying around Heaven," Jack said. "Said all these angels were flying with him. He said they hugged him and whispered all kinds of uplifting stuff. You couldn't wipe the grin off his face. Before I helped him to the bedroom back there, he said he *talked* to God."

"Lucky bastard. *I'm* the one who needs to talk to God because I've got a shitload of questions—and some constructive criticism."

"Well, at least *you're* back to normal," Jack said with a mild smile that hinted at either worry or fatigue from witnessing the insanity of the night. "Well, your version of *normal* abnormal anyway."

"Mornin'," a bright-eyed JD said as he emerged from the bedroom.

"Well, look who put his harp down to mingle with us heathens," I said.

"That was the craziest night of my life," JD announced. "Thanks, Uncle Ben."

"I knew I should've listened to Nancy Reagan about drugs," I said. "I keep being a bad influence."

"No, no, no," he said as he placed his hand on my shoulder. He knew I was not even touchy-feely with extended family. "For the first time in my life, it's all good. My whole life folks have been talking about religious experiences and feeling God's presence. Until last night, I was a believer but not a *true* believer. Now, I get it. I have never felt that warmth, that glowing love from above. And, I *know* there are angels among us. I even saw angel children. I *held* one...in my arms. She was so beautiful. It was the most amazing thing I have ever experienced in my entire life."

A lone tear streamed from the corner of his eye toward his smiling lips.

"Jesus," I said as I rubbed my hands through what was left of my hair. "Look, I'm glad your trip went better than my nightmare, but it was just that—*a trip*. Maybe there's something folks can get out of this weird-ass stinky medicine man potion, but nothing from last night was real."

"Pickin' and grinnin' with Lucas Parsons?" JD asked with a worried look.

"Oh, that was definitely real," Jack assured him. "And it was pretty awesome."

"To me, *that* was like that was a dream, and the so-called trip last night was more real," JD noted, believing that he had just come up with a profound observation. "Whatever happened, it *changed* me. I'm...different. I'm *better* than I was yesterday. I'm loved. I'm safe. I'm forgiven. I'm—"

"Insane?" I suggested. JD just smiled and squeezed my shoulder again. "Ugh," I sighed as I pulled away.

"We probably should get back to the campground," Jack noted.

"Yeah, let's hurry," JD said. "I was going to skip church today, but I've changed my mind. I gotta get cleaned up. I've heard Mom, Dad, all these folks at church, at school, talk about having a religious experience, and I never had one worth talking about until now."

"Can you leave out the part about the ayahuasca—and me?" I asked.

"Sure, Uncle Ben. You don't have to believe me, but I *know* that God has been working through you all along to get to me. That's why you invited me here last night. Now I understand that, yes, He works in mysterious ways, even through crazy uncles like you."

I turned to Jack. "Is there a mule or something around here that can kick him in the head and get him back to normal?"

"To be honest with both of you, I've sorta lost track of what's normal," Jack said. "I think I need some quiet time. Maybe I'll do a little writing today."

"Oh boy. We're gonna look mighty bad in this *Gone with the Fried Green Crawdads* sociology report of yours, ain't we?" I asked. "Well, me anyway."

"I've definitely learned more in the past few weeks than in the previous eighteen years," he said.

"Is that good or bad?" I asked earnestly.

"I'd rather have understanding than a lack of it," he said. "You know, we still haven't sat down for our official interview. I've only got a couple more weeks before I head...home."

"Hey, man," JD said as he placed his hand on Jack's shoulder this time. "When *you're* here, this is home, too. Now, we gotta run. You wanna go to church with me?"

"I'm gonna sit this one out," Jack said matter-of-factly.

There was hope for the kid, after all, I thought. But he still had some explaining to do.

# THE GIRL ON THE FRONT PORCH SWING

I stayed in the cabin for another hour after the boys left. I was drained. I felt like I'd just escaped from a month of captivity in a jungle country's civil war instead of having a taste of Peruvian peace that Daniel had suggested I might experience, and I damn sure didn't feel enlightened. Sorry, Aaron Rodgers, but I'll pass—no pun intended.

In addition to feeling anxious after running from demons all night, I was confused by the bond being cemented by JD and Jack. I'd known JD for eighteen years, yet he seemed as close—if not *closer*—to Jack, who had been there all of four weeks. I doubted there were any sociology studies going on and wondered if the kid was even a real college student.

I dropped by Daniel's house to thank him for the generous invite to the awful night. He had seen a handful of folks endure bad trips and understood.

"I hate that, brother," he told me. "Guess I'm guilty of projecting my positive trips. I need to stop that. I just wish you—I wish *everyone*—could feel what I get out of it, that overwhelming sense of peace."

"Dude, I'd settle for a *sliver* of peace," I said. "By the way, are the other fellas gone?"

"Yep. They all hit the road early. Oh, but Lucas left this note for your nephew and the other kid."

"JD and Jack," I noted.

"Yeah, I didn't read it, but he was very impressed with their little performance last night, especially the kid from up North. We all were. I think he wants to invite him to visit his studio or something. Maybe he thinks he's discovered somebody."

"Well, he certainly has my permission," I said with the closest thing to a smile that I could muster. "Good seeing you again, Daniel. This place is beautiful and plenty peaceful without that devil tea. Not a big fan of the dudes painted on the walls, though. Fast little fuckers, though. Chased me all night."

"They're not so bad once you get to know them," he said with a chuckle. "Take it easy, Ben. Go find some peace in the Holler."

"Haven't found it yet, but today's a new day, right?"

"I've never had a *today* that had already happened, so you might be right. Adios, amigo."

"Au revoir."

* * *

I kept the radio off during the fifteen-minute drive back to Possum Holler. My brain couldn't endure more stimulation. In fact, I decided then and there to take a break from drinking and gummies. I didn't know how long it might last. A month? A week? An hour and a half? I just needed a break from *everything*.

Besides, I wanted to be sober and clear-headed the next time I talked to Jack. The kid was hiding something, and I planned to drag the truth out of him. If necessary, I could summon my inner redneck and scare it out of him.

That conversation would have to wait, though, because a gray Ford Escape was sitting in my driveway, and someone was sitting in my front porch swing when I arrived. I crouched behind the wheel and squinted. Who in the hell had the audacity to plop down in my swing? The person then looked up, and I knew that face. I saw it all the time in my sleep. I briefly saw it peeking over the wall the previous night.

"Welcome home," I said as I stepped out of the truck and meandered her way. I could tell by the wince on her face that I'd already triggered Riley—not a difficult feat.

"You know this isn't home for me. Oh, by the way, there's a guy in my apartment."

"How can it be your apartment if...never mind. Name's Jack. He's staying a couple more weeks this summer. I'm renting it out. Sorry I didn't mention it in one of the chats we haven't had recently."

"Don't worry," she said. "I met him as soon as he got out of the shower. He seemed pretty decent for a wet naked guy."

"Actually he and your cousin have gotten pretty close the past few weeks," I said.

"Yeah, that's what he said."

"Well, he hasn't told me much. You probably know more than I do."

"Speaking of things you don't know—" Riley stood up and put her hands on her hips, framing her slightly protruding belly.

"What the—"

"A little more than three months," she said matter-of-factly.

"I need to sit down." Riley just stood there with her pregnant self while I plopped down on the front steps and stared off toward the quiet Highway 128. "What are you going to do?"

"Um, I'm having a baby," she said. I couldn't see her face, but I knew she was rolling her eyes. "I didn't come here to tell you that."

"Oh, good! There's *more*?"

"I just came to get the last of my stuff—you know, the stuff that *was* in my apartment. I didn't come to talk about *this*."

"Why all of the sudden do you need your stuff that's just been sitting there for a year?"

"We're moving."

"We who? You and the daddy?"

"No, I'm going with Mom and Roger."

"And they're going—?"

"To London."

I turned my head and glared at her. "What do you know about London? What do you know about being a parent?"

"Well, I know how *not* to be a parent. And I've been to London several times over the past year or so. Look, I just came to get my stuff, but I don't know where it is."

"So, this has been coming for a while? Damn, I am so in the dark."

"That's an understatement," she said.

I was too drained emotionally, physically, spiritually, to deliver a comeback.

"Riley, I love you," I whined. "All those play dates in the park, all the books we read, the movies we watched together, awful shit that I laughed at because you were laughing, the times we went to—"

"I don't recall *any* of that, but, you know, if it helps you deal with the ramifications of your actions, dragging us down to this hillbilly hellhole, by all means, remember away."

"You know what's worse than amnesia?" I asked rhetorically before answering my own question: "A shared memory that's no longer shared. Those wonderful memories—they hurt like hell now. I used to treasure them. Now, they haunt me. Every day. Every goddamn day. Your stuff's boxed up in the bonus room."

"Thanks."

* * *

God, how I longed for a drink. It was too early, though, and I had no idea what kind of demons tequila might conjure up on the heels of an ayahuasca trip—a journey I would never be taking again. It may have brought Mucho Loco to Shangri-la and JD to Jesus, but it dragged me to the gates of hell, which I apparently ran circles around all night long. I was irritated, and it felt like the perfect frame of mind for me to finally corner Jack and find out what the hell was going on behind my back—or in front of my clueless eyes. Jack opened the door just before I could knock.

"I was just about to go looking for you," he said.

"I'm ready for you and I to have our sit-down now," I told him. "In fact, I may have more questions for you than you do for me."

"It may have to wait," he said somberly.

"The hell it will!"

"A lady came by a little while ago," he said.

"Yeah, Riley's back, but not for long," I said.

"No," Jack said. "I did meet Riley. Nice girl."

"So I'm told."

"Someone else came by. Shantae. Shantae Bailey. She was pretty upset."

"That's Travis' daughter, from the place that got hit by the tornado."

"Yeah, I don't know how to tell you this, but Travis passed away yesterday. She said he had a massive heart attack."

"Damn," I said with a sigh as I looked up at the gray morning sky as if to ask the non-existent big guy upstairs if he was done torturing folks in my neck of the woods. "I know he wasn't the healthiest guy around but, geez, I didn't see that coming."

"She said they think it's broken-heart syndrome," Jack said.

"Sounds like bullshit. I suspect it's fried chicken and liquor syndrome."

"Actually, there *is* such a thing," Jack argued.

"As fried chicken and liquor? Yes, I'm well aware. Have you met me?"

"No, broken-heart syndrome."

"Is that some BS you learned in *sociology*?" I asked using air quotes. "If you could die of a broken heart, I'd be long gone, kid. Besides, I had a real heart attack about five years ago. Whatever the *widow maker* artery is was 99 percent blocked."

"I'm guessing you survived?"

"Near as I can tell. Sometimes I wish it'd been a hundred percent blocked and taken me out while Riley still loved me. Wait. Why am I telling you this? What did Shantae need?"

"She just wanted to let you know before you heard it somewhere else, and she said she wanted to thank you for treating her daddy like a friend when everybody else was looking down on him."

"That poor girl," I said while rubbing my head. "Losing her daddy right after losing her little girl. Losing a child, man, that's tough to handle."

"Apparently, he and her little girl were very close," Jack noted.

"Yeah, I don't think the daddy was involved, and I know Shantae worked a couple of jobs. Travis and that little girl probably spent a lot of time together. Poor guy. Way to go, Jesus!" I yelled sarcastically as I glanced back up at the heavens. "I think they've had enough, and they're the most Christian folks I know! Quit Job'n them!"

"She said you were the only white person around here who treated her family with respect."

"It wasn't some white-black thing," I said. "Travis and I had gone to school together since kindergarten. We were just friends and classmates, and there were plenty of white and black kids who were friends when they were very young. Over the years, back then anyway, folks gradually drifted into their camps—including racial. In fact, I think Travis saw me as white more than I saw him as black. I know he took some heat from his black friends for hanging around a white guy that they saw as rich, even though we were just middle-class folks."

"Thank goodness times have changed," Jack said.

"Somewhat, but not as much as you might think," I said. "It's just a little more under the surface. It's not polite or decent to be racist or openly prejudiced, so if you are, you gotta keep it to yourself or within the walls of your home. You've got to pretend you don't notice color when you're out and about."

"But *you* don't notice color," he argued. "Travis knew that."

"Of course, I notice color! Hell, my daughter—my beautiful daughter who hates me—is half-black. You think I don't notice that? I notice when people have blonde hair or red hair, whether they're short or tall. It's not about being colorblind or not seeing differences—it's all about how you treat other people regardless of what they look like or what differences you have."

"Very Christian of you," he noted with a wry smile.

"I am kind of into that love-thy-neighbor thing. You know, me and Jesus are simpatico. American Christians and Jesus, not so much. Speaking of which, I need to get cleaned up and get some food to take out there."

"Is that a Christian thing, too?" Jack asked.

"No, it's a Southern thing. You die, we eat. Get married, we eat. Graduate, we eat. There's no life event that doesn't warrant a box of fried chicken or a bunch of pig-in-a-blankets."

"You mean *pigs*-in-a-blanket," he corrected.

"You the grammar police?"

"Pork police."

"You need help. You going with?"

"I don't think they need strangers visiting right now," he said. "Probably better if it's just friends and family."

"Then be a new friend. Besides, we gotta talk, and I don't know a better place to do it than in the truck."

"Why's that?" he asked.

"In case I get the urge to push you out on the road somewhere."

"You might."

"I was afraid of that. Clean yourself up, and get ready. We got shit to do."

* * *

Riley could not have had many "things" to gather while I was showering and dressing in jeans and a short-sleeved knit shirt that was as close as I was willing to get to formal wear. In fact, when I walked out of the house, she was leaning against my truck and chatting with Jack, who smiled and nodded as he pushed his still damp dark bangs out of his eyes. At least Riley was willing to talk to *someone*. I knew I'd better not rock the boat as my lines into Riley's world had been going dead for a while—and it would be more important to know what was going on in Riley's life over the upcoming months than it had been for the past couple of years. There was, possibly, another person to consider. I certainly was not privy to her plans—which I knew were more likely written in the clouds than in stone.

"Heading out?" I asked.

"Actually, JD and I are going to hang out for a little bit as soon as he gets out of church. Then I'm going home."

"Uh-huh," I mumbled. "Well, I love you, and I sure hope you keep me updated on, um, *things*." I glanced at her stomach and then back into her eyes.

"We'll see," she said before giving Jack a quick hug and hopping into the driver's seat of the Escape.

"You," I said as I turned my glare to Jack. "Time to talk. Get in."

* * *

After we picked up a box of fried chicken from the Americus Wal-Mart—the only place I could think of to get anything to take to the Baileys on a Sunday—Jack explained that he was indeed in Possum Holler on a learning mission. However, it had more to do with himself and very little to do with the South.

He said he had loving, open-minded parents who adopted him as an infant. His birth mother gave him up for adoption in Rhode Island, where it was easier for him to track down information about his birth and his mother. With the services of someone he called a "search angel," he found his mother's name and last known address.

"You know, there was a time when I was in school in Rhode Island that I didn't hear from my sister for a year or two," I said.

"That was when she was still wild, before she moved back here and settled down with the preacher man. Please don't tell me you're my nephew. Don't tell me Sarah's your mother."

"Not exactly," he said while looking out the passenger-side window.

"But you're down here looking for your mother, right?"

"No, she died years ago. Car wreck. In California. About all I know is her name was Natalie and she was a folk singer and poet. She claimed she didn't know who my father was. She died in a single-car accident. Hit a tree. That was all while I was a baby."

"A few decades late to become the next Joni Mitchell, but maybe that explains your musical talent. Wait, if she died, then what the hell are you doing here?"

"I came to see my brother," he said in a near-whisper.

"And?"

"He's a great guy."

I slammed the brakes, and the truck skidded off Highway 49 and onto a grassy shoulder bordering a pecan orchard. The front of my truck slammed one of the rickety wooden posts holding up a stretch of rusty barbed wire and knocked it down. The box of fried chicken flew off the backseat and into the rear floorboard.

"You said Sarah's *not* your mom!" I yelled. "What the fuck?! What the actual fuck?!"

"She's not, I swear!" After a pause, he mumbled, "But JD *is* my brother. He was adopted, too. There's more."

"WHAT?"

"When's JD's birthday?" he asked.

"October..." I had to think for a moment, "ninth. Yeah. I remember because it's John Lennon's birthday, too."

"It's also mine. Imagine that. We're twins." I looked at him disbelievingly. "*Fraternal* twins."

"But you're in college and he just graduated high school."

"I guess October birthdays fall into that in-between zone of when you should start school."

I kept both hands on the steering wheel and stared straight ahead.

"You sure about all this?"

"A hundred percent."

"Does JD know?" I asked.

"No."

"Does Sarah know?"

"No."

"Cool. Now, get the fuck out!"

"What?"

"You're a liar and a fraud! Get the fuck out of my truck, pack your shit, and leave! Go back to Boston or wherever you're really from. Who knows what's true anymore?!"

"You're gonna leave me here in the middle of nowhere?"

"*Everywhere* around here's the middle of nowhere! Ain't you figured that out?!"

"How am I gonna get back to the apartment to get my stuff, my car?" he asked bewilderedly as he stepped out of the truck.

"I don't know. Call your brother. Hell, call Riley. Clearly, she'll talk to you. She'll talk to any damn body but me."

"I'd rather not disturb them right now," he said. "I think they're having a picnic. She said they had some catching up to do."

"Well, God forbid you rock the boat or disturb the peace around here!" I rubbed my head and spoke with a quieter resignation. "Look, JD's more like a son than a nephew to me, even more so since Riley left. Now, I find out he's not even my nephew. Jesus Christ. Damn, have I got anything left?"

"Oh, come off it! He's the same kid today he was yesterday. He's just as much your nephew as he's ever been. Hell, he's more your nephew than he is my brother."

"That's because he doesn't know. He can't handle it, Jack. I don't know what kind of shit is mixing around in his head, but it's been going on for months. It was subtle, though—until that baseball game. Now he's climbing balconies at the beach to fight strangers, seeing angels, and talking to Jesus. He can't handle this right now. He's teetering like he's in a chair balancing on its back legs. He could fall a little forward or a lot backwards in an instant. He's just gotta keep that balance until all these recent events blow over and become blips in his story someday."

"Actually, if he knew—"

"No! You're *not* telling him, and you're not telling Sarah, either. If she ever did want him to know the truth, I'm damn sure it's not a truth bomb she wants to drop on him right now—especially since they believe he's started finding himself and Jesus again and embarking upon some righteous path. I know they've been nice to you, kid, but Sarah has been suppressing her *own* demons for a long, long time. Remember, I was once the good child. *She* was the wild heathen. If you throw this stick of dynamite into her safe, little churchy world, she could unleash all kinds of hell on you—and on me. Worse, it could destroy JD."

"I just want to know why—" he whimpered.

"Why what?"

"Why we were split up, why she didn't adopt us both. Why did she choose JD and not me?"

"I'm warning you, kid, don't do it. She might snap and kill you."

"And you?"

"I'd love to kill you, but that ain't my thing. Hard truths might not be my thing, either. Apparently, neither is family. Not that I have any left."

"One thing I *have* learned," he said as he leaned in through the open passenger-side window, "is that family is not only about blood."

"You know where to get your stuff," I said matter-of-factly.

"Do I?"

"Yonder way," I said while pointing northwest. "About seven or eight miles. I'd get going if I were you. If Snake Simmons sees you standing here at his tore-up fence, he just might load your ass up with buckshot. On second thought, maybe you should stay here. Get comfortable."

I backed the truck off the post and sped down 49 toward the Baileys' tornado-ravaged acres of despair with a floorboard of chicken.

# The Thinking Spot

I don't know if there's a five-second rule for picking up fried chicken from a pickup truck floorboard, but it's not like fried chicken can get *unhealthier*, so I shoved the pieces back into the box as soon as I reached the drive to the Bailey compound. Though the temperature outside was approaching the boiling point, I lowered the windows in the cab of the truck in hopes that the dusty wind along that dirt road would take away some of the greasy air. Instead, it made my truck smell dirty *and* greasy.

A large group of folks gathered on and around Travis' front porch. Out of the corner of my eye, I could see Shantae in the family cemetery, a couple hundred feet from the house. I made the rounds with the mourners but did not say much other than, "I'm so sorry." I had a lot of recent experience with stirring up troubles, but I was less skilled at easing them. I left them the floorboard chicken and walked toward Shantae.

She was kneeling at the grave of her daughter, which had yet to get a permanent gravestone—just a simple wooden cross with Imani's name and birth and death dates. I approached Shantae from the side so that she could see me without being startled. She glanced my way, wiped a tear, and gave a half-hearted smile.

"Thanks for coming, Mr. Ben."

"Of course," was all I could spit out. "Ben is fine."

"Daddy used to talk about how y'all played together as kids," she said as she stood to face me. "He said you were different from most white folks around here."

"I'm afraid I may be different from most folks, period, not that it's necessarily a good thing."

"You know, whenever I worked at Muckalee Christian, cleaning the bathrooms and everything, you were the only person there who ever smiled at me or asked me how I was doing. I appreciate that."

"Sorry, I didn't know they treated you like that," I said. "If it makes you feel any better, they *hate* me over there now."

"They didn't treat me good or bad. They just kinda ignored me. I was like...wallpaper or invisible. And, yes, I heard about you losing your job. I'm sorry."

"I appreciate that, but I'm not sorry. I thought I could pretend to be something I'm not long enough to help those kids become decent adults someday. I thought I could justify not being true to myself if the result was good. It weighs on you, though. Did you say when you *worked* at the school?"

"Yeah, I quit last week," Shantae said. "It's not like there's a whole lot of cleaning to do during summer break anyway. Besides, I didn't want to be their wallpaper anymore. I figured if y'all can make a stand like y'all did at that game that *everybody* was talking about, I could, too."

"I didn't know you knew about that," I said.

"I don't know exactly what happened, but I got the gist of it. Daddy thought it was funny, but he wasn't surprised."

"Well, I certainly wouldn't have wanted you to lose your job," I said.

"I've still got Waffle House, and it's not hard to find cleaning work or waitress jobs around here," she said. "Besides, who am I making money for? Imani's gone. Daddy's gone."

She threw her arms around my shoulders and began sobbing into my chest. There was nothing to say. I just held her until she could regain her composure. When she pulled away, I had a question.

"You came by the house earlier?" I asked. "You need something? If there's *anything* you need, just let me know."

"Actually, I came by to drop something off," she said. "But I didn't know the boy there and figured I'd better wait. Come with me."

We walked back to her daddy's house and into the room where Shantae slept, a room she once shared with Imani. On the nightstand was a stack of envelopes.

"Your mail was piling up in the school office, so I snuck it out for you on my way out the door."

"I appreciate it," I said. "It was unnecessary, probably a bunch of junk, but that was very sweet of you."

"Well, you never know," she said. "Thanks again, Mr. Ben, for everything." She wrapped her arms around me once again, and I gently held her.

"Mm-hmmph." The throat-clearing sound came from one of Travis' uncles whose name I couldn't remember, though the glare on his face was familiar. Some of the older folks in the Bailey family never trusted any white people. I understood, given what they had witnessed in the Jim Crow years before I was born. I didn't try to win them over, but I was kind. Hugging Travis' daughter, however, no matter how innocent, was too much for the relative to take.

"It's family time now," he said gruffly. "Thanks for the chicken."

"Again," I said softly to both, "I'm so sorry for your loss."

"Uh-huh."

I grabbed my stack of mail and wound through the crowd. Some nodded in appreciation, while a few others simply stared in disbelief that a white person had come to pay his respects. I wanted to say, "Hey, I'm one of the decent ones," but that seemed inappropriate at the moment.

I hopped in the truck and tossed the mail onto the passenger seat. Most of it appeared to be the usual wastes of paper from insurance companies and school associations, but one letter stood out because it was handwritten with the return address:

Jenny Jacobs

113 Willow Lake Road
Thomasville GA 31757

* * *

By 5 p.m., it was more than 100 degrees, above average even for mid-July. I sat back in my Adirondack chair and let the sun fry my face and scalp, which got more sun with each passing year as my hair thinned. I was ready to shave it down to almost nothing but had not made the time. In prior years, when I still had a shred of vanity left, I dared not shave it for fear that my head might be even uglier and whiter than I suspected, perhaps even Uncle Fester-like. Now, I no longer cared. In one hand, I carefully raised a cup to my lips while I drummed the fingers of my right hand on the armrest. I heard a vehicle coming up the driveway and then the shutting of a door. The scrunch of footsteps on the mix of gravel and dirt of my driveway replaced the sound of the vehicle pulling away.

"I thought you weren't going to drink today. You trade tequila for beer? What kind?"

"Root," I said. "*Diet* Root to be exact. You know I'm a health nut. I thought you were stranded in the middle of nowhere, so I was celebrating. How'd you get here anyway?"

"Believe it or not," Jack said as he plopped down into the other Adirondack chair, "I got an Uber."

"Rub some cream on it," I said. My sarcastic sense of humor was forced and landed with a thud as Jack said nothing. "Well, congratulations on being the first person Uber'd into Possum Holler. That'll be quite the accomplishment as you're leaving."

"I'll be heading out soon, I promise," he said.

"You're right about that."

Jack turned his attention to the envelope sitting on the small iron end table beside my chair. "Is that my eviction notice?"

"No, if I notice you haven't evicted yourself soon, then you'll notice your ass getting kicked." He was not buying the bluster. "Actually, speaking of ass-kickings—"

"Huh?"

"Remember that day in Panama City when I showed up with my face all jacked up?"

"When you got your ass kicked in a dream? Yeah, not exactly the kind of thing that slips your mind. What about it?"

"Apparently, I really did get my ass whupped the night before," I said as I picked up the envelope and tapped it on the armrest. "This letter is from the woman I saw down there at the campground, someone I met almost forty years ago if you can believe that. Getting my ass whupped in a dream seemed more plausible."

"Wow, what's the letter say?"

"One, it's none of your business, *stranger*," I told him as I stared sternly into his eyes. "Two, I haven't opened it. Maybe it's an apology. Maybe it's a love letter from 1990. Maybe she thinks she can get me a better deal on car insurance. Maybe I'm being sued for injuring her ex's fist with my face. I don't know."

"Well, there's a way to find—"

"Don't, kid," I warned him. "You accomplished your mission. You found your brother and found out he's a great kid. A little confused, perhaps, but who's not?"

"I promise you, Ben, that JD *needs* to know. He's *got* to know. You've got to trust me on this one, for his sake."

"*Trust* you?" I sarcastically laughed at the concept. "Damn, kid, you've got some balls on that skinny little frame of yours to be talking about *trust*."

"If he knew—"

"No!" I yelled as I rose from my chair and thrust my finger in his face.

"I'm just saying it would take a huge burden off his shoulders, a burden he doesn't have to tote."

"How?"

"I just know. I don't *believe* it. I know it."

"Don't you have some packing to do?"

"Yeah," he said with heavy resignation in his voice. "I'll do that. I'll leave a lovely review of my stay."

"Hell, you can give it *zero* stars if you want," I said matter-of-factly. "It'd be a lie, but you seem pretty comfortable with that.

Besides, the apartment's no longer available—and it never will be again."

* * *

While Jack packed, I got out of the sun and plopped down in my den's recliner. My plan was to watch the news before the Braves appeared on Sunday Night Baseball. By six o'clock, I'd fallen asleep, although my snores kept jolting me awake. I still had drunk no alcohol nor swallowed a gummy. After that wild Saturday night, the last thing I needed was help dozing off. Perhaps there was some trace of ayahuasca in my system. I still ain't exactly sure what it is and don't care. Unfortunately, I kept bumping into the same demon dudes from Daniel's weird wall in my dreams. It was an hourlong cycle of conking out, getting chased again, and then snoring myself back to the relative safety of the real world. I wanted to rest, but I also wanted to steer clear of the colorful creeps. I tried to force myself to keep my eyes open so that I might be able to hit the sack at a reasonable hour and get some much-needed rest, more so for my brain than my body. Then, yet again, my eyelids closed for what seemed like a millisecond, and they came after me. Instead of my snores saving me this time, I was rescued by the "Sanford and Son" ringtone of my phone. I downloaded it because I loved the song, but, in retrospect, it was a jarring choice for a ringtone during sleepy time. I damn near fell out of the recliner trying to grab my phone away from the dream freaks. The caller ID, though, was even scarier—“Sis.”

“Dammit!” I yelled before answering, “Yeah?”

“Is JD there?”

“I’m sorry, what?”

“JD said he was going to have a snack with Riley and hasn’t come home,” she said. “He’s not answering his phone. Ben, I know we’ve got issues, but I’m worried.”

“I haven’t seen him, Sarah, and I don’t know where Riley is—not that she’d tell me.”

“Why is she here anyway?” Sarah asked.

Though she had never vocalized it, I knew she was no fan of Elizabeth. It wasn’t racial—at least I don’t *think* it was—but it was more Elizabeth’s artistic nature and liberal learnings that turned Sis off. She had told me more than once that she feared Elizabeth would hurt me. She was damn sure right about that. I think she saw too much of Elizabeth in Riley. Now that I think about it, maybe she also saw too much of *me* in Riley. Regardless, she certainly didn’t like that Riley and JD had always been more like best friends than cousins. There was no way I’d reveal what Riley had told—well, *showed*—me hours earlier.

“She just came to pick up the last of her stuff,” I said.

“How about, uh, what’s-his-name?”

“Jack.”

"Yeah."

"He's leaving, too," I said. "Something came up at home, I reckon."

"Something weird is going on, Ben," she said. "I just know it. JD was in such a good mood this morning and at church. He's been doing so much better lately. He hasn't been this happy in months."

"Because he hasn't spent much time with me lately?"

"Maybe, but that's not the point," she argued. "Ben, I need your help. I just need to know he's OK. If he's still out with Riley, that's fine, but I need to know."

"OK," I relented. "I'll catch Jack before he heads out and see if he's heard anything. I'll call if I find out anything."

I hate talking on the phone, whether it's to a telemarketer, friend, or family, so I texted JD. I could hear Riley's rental car coming up the drive as I waited for the message to show that it was delivered and read. Neither occurred. As I waited for a reply, I could hear faint chatting from outside. Great, I thought. Jack had made yet another friend, the daughter who hated me. How in the hell could he weave himself so easily into people's lives and be so welcomed, while I was a pariah in my own community and even in my own family? I tried to call JD, but it went straight to voicemail:

"Hey, you've reached JD. Leave a message, and I'll get back to you as soon as possible. God bless."

"God bless? When the hell did he change that?" I wondered aloud.

I donned my OK-to-get-dirty sneakers by the back door in case I needed to help track down JD, though I was certain Sarah was overreacting. He was eighteen, after all. Most of the times he *disappeared* in Possum Holler, he could be found at the same place. It likely was where he and Riley had their afternoon meeting. For all of his efforts to fit in and go along with the crowd through the years, he had another side that few of us witnessed save for a few gators at his so-called Thinking Spot underneath the old railroad trestle where it crossed Timber Creek, which ultimately wound its way to the Flint not far from Riverside Free Will in the Cutoff. Gators aren't much for conversation, and they'll let you reflect all you want unless you have food or a small cocker spaniel with you. JD's Thinking Spot had been my fishing spot as a kid, and I suspect some of those same gators were still there. Hell, some of them probably had barely moved in forty years. Of course, the fishing sucked directly under those trestles, so I carved out a path through the years to a couple of backwaters where I could pull out a few bluegill, shellcrackers and catfish whenever I needed my own quiet time at JD's age. I don't recall doing a lot of thinking down there, though. Reflection wasn't exactly my specialty as a kid—or as an adult—which may explain how I wound up stranded in my Possum Holler kingdom that was supposed to be our home sweet home. The only thing that might have made JD find another spot for his outing with Riley would be that he had discovered days earlier that the narrow dirt path through which he could barely navigate his truck down to the creek was littered with fallen trees from the recent tornado. That's why he and Jack wound up picking Whitewater for their camping spot instead of the sandbar near the trestle.

As I opened the door, I saw Riley and Jack engaged in polite conversation yet again. I overheard the last bit:

"It's definitely been a learning experience," he said. "Good folks, and *great* food. But I don't fit in."

"Tell me about it," Riley said before hearing the door shut behind me. She then turned back to Jack and gave him a hug that seemed a little too friendly for a couple of relative strangers. "Fitting in is overrated. If you're ever in New York, give me a call. We'll do lunch or something."

"Sounds good," Jack said meekly, noting the tension between me and the person I loved more than anyone on the planet.

"I'm heading out," she told me.

"Before you go," I started, prompting a familiar rolling of the eyes, "do you know where JD is?"

"Why?"

"Because your Aunt Sarah's looking for him and can't get hold of him."

"Sorry," she said as she glanced toward the ground. "I don't know. I thought he was heading home. Tell her not to worry. I'm sure he's fine. I've got a plane to catch in Atlanta."

"All right," I said with obvious resignation that I didn't try to hide.

Riley tossed a satchel into the back seat of her rental and opened the driver door. As she began to close the door, I shouted, "I love you!"

There was no response, only the cranking of the engine. Almost as quickly as Riley had come, she was gone. Jack timidly tried to sneak into his apartment undetected.

"Hey!" I yelled. "What about you? You seen JD?"

"No, sorry. Something wrong?"

"His mom's just worried, but she's a worrier," I said. "Why? *Should* something be wrong? Is there something *else* you're not telling me?"

"Nothing you don't already know," he said sheepishly.

"What the hell does that mean?!" I no longer felt that Sarah's concern was completely unjustified. Jack was nervous, and *that* unnerved me.

"Last night, this morning. You said all these demons or whatever chasing you felt real, right?"

"Yeah. And?"

"JD's experience felt very real, too. I didn't do the stuff. I witnessed it. It was more real than you know."

"Well, I sure hate I missed a bunch of real live angels falling from the sky! I could have finally had my religious experience instead of being chased by demons all night long! That's super helpful. Thanks."

"I just know at least one part of it was—*is*—very real, all too real. And I'm pretty sure I know where he is right now."

"His Thinking Spot?"

"Yeah."

"Good work, Sherlock. The place he goes every time he needs to get away from all the craziness around here—who else could've ever figured that out?" Jack ignored me and began touching the screen of his phone with his index finger. "Don't bother. I've already tried texting. He's not answering. I think his phone's cut off. And that spot is probably hard to get to with all the downed trees from the tornado."

"Maybe," he said. "But, yeah, he's definitely at that spot. Well, at least that's definitely the last place he was."

"How do you know?" I asked.

"We're sharing each other's location on the phone," he explained. "We did it when we got back from Panama City, after we had to go looking for him that day. Look." Jack held his phone screen so I could see it.

"Well, that's *near* his so-called Thinking Spot," I said. "But it's like halfway down that path from the highway."

"It's the last known location," Jack said. "And it's not moving."

"Hell, it'd be faster to walk the tracks down to there," I said. "You can finish packing. I'll be back shortly. If I were you, I'd be rolling toward Boston by then."

"I'm going with you," Jack insisted, causing the veins in my temple to bulge and throb.

"I ain't got time for liars, kid. You know I'm usually a laid-back guy, but I swear to you: If you follow me down those tracks, you won't come back. It's been a long twenty-four hours, and my head is already killing me. Besides, this is *family* business." I fully intended for that to sting.

"I *am* family!" Jack yelled.

"Not mine! Pack your shit and get the hell out of here! I'll refund your whole damn stay! Just go home! Write your book or your school report or turn us into the crazy police! Just fucking leave!"

Jack stormed back to his apartment and slammed the door behind him. I wanted to ring his scrawny little neck for disrespecting my property after all that had happened and as hospitable as I'd been since day one. But he had never exhibited any behavior like this before, and I worried that he would be in there furiously redialing JD to tell him the family secret that I believed would utterly devastate JD—that JD was adopted and they were brothers. I knew Jack earnestly believed knowing the truth would somehow benefit JD, but I was certain it would do the opposite. I walked briskly west toward the tracks and marched deliberately along the timbers. I could hear the faint starting of a car engine from back at the house.

"That little bastard!" I yelled aloud. I knew he had not finished packing. He was not going home. He was on a mission to beat me to JD. I stepped up my pace.

As concerned as I was about JD's well-being, I also was terrified that I might have just seen my daughter for the final time, a feeling I'd had before and one that worsened with each parting. Riley's earlier insistence on taking a semester off to backpack across Europe seemed downright responsible compared to her current predicament. She's just crazy enough to think she could be a parent, I thought. I had everything it took to be a good parent and desperately tried to give Riley the foundation for her to grow, thrive, succeed, and be happy, but it blew up in my face. Good intentions don't guarantee success in raising kids.

I didn't expect her to go through with having this baby, but, then again, it would be just like her to embrace such a decision, even more so if she thought I might not support it. Time was running out for her to have a decision to make. With Elizabeth and her new moneybags husband there to bail her out of any situation or to financially back any leap of faith, I knew I had to be careful how I reacted because any false step might ensure that

I indeed just saw my daughter for the final time. As long as there was an ounce of hope that we could come to a truce in the future, I wouldn't blow it up. I had no influence over her, and she had no love for me. I was in no position to do anything but wait and hope for the best. It was not even an ounce of hope, more like a gram. Still, I parked that speck of hope somewhere in my weak and broken heart and clung to it with all the fortitude I could muster.

That broken heart of mine began to throb the closer I got to the trestle, partly from worry but also from not having exercised in months. OK, *years*. A passing train gave me a moment to step off the tracks and catch my breath. I had only another couple hundred yards to go before I would be able to see the path that led down to JD's creekside Thinking Spot near the trestle. As I returned to the tracks for the final stretch, I heard the familiar rumbling and clacking of the train wheels on the trestle over Timber Creek. As those sounds grew softer, a shrill scream pierced the peace. It was a male voice. I hoped no one had a "Stand By Me" moment on the trestle that I'd stupidly crossed more than once as a boy. I began to jog. The screams grew louder. Finally, I could make out the sound.

"JD!"

I raced down the old path to the creek with overgrown branches slapping my face and stubborn briars snagging my legs that were bloodied by the time I reached the clearing at the

Thinking Spot. Jack was on his hands and knees. He pounded the muddy creekbank, splattering brown muck against his clothes. From a high timber supporting the tracks above, JD twisted to and fro on a rope with a noose brutally cutting into his bent neck.

"JD died. Please tell Riley. She does not want to hear it from me. He killed himself."

That's the text I sent Elizabeth after returning home from the creek. She immediately called. It was the first time we had spoken in months.

"Oh my God, Ben! What the hell?"

"I don't know," I muttered. "This morning was the happiest I've ever seen him."

"Did Riley see him?" she asked.

"Yeah, earlier this afternoon."

"What are we gonna do, Ben? This will devastate Riley."

Her use of the word "we" pissed me off, but I was in no mood to point out that I'd been abandoned by her and then Riley, not to mention completely shut out of both of their lives. "How is Sarah?"

"How would you be if you lost your only child?" I asked, somewhat rhetorically.

"I can't imagine."

"I *can* imagine," I said. Elizabeth was silent. "Look, just get in touch with Riley. I'm sure she's at the Atlanta airport by now, hopefully through security. I'm scared for her—"

"and the baby," she finished.

"And what the hell is that all about?! Is she really going through with having a baby? At her age?"

"It's her decision, and we'll support her in whatever she decides."

"Well, she'd better decide pretty damn quick because—you know what? I can't deal with that right now. She won't listen to me anyway."

"I just don't understand why JD would do something so crazy."

"I know," I sighed. "Look, I gotta go."

"Please call me if you—"

I assumed she wanted me to get back in touch when I learned more, but I couldn't take hearing another word from her. Besides, I now had an idea what might've triggered JD, but I was angry with him for what I believed was an extreme overreaction. Unlike JD, I didn't care what folks thought of me. I had let plenty of people down through the years, though not intentionally. I had no doubt the prospect of letting people down mixed with the internal guilt was what led JD to the end of his rope.

Jack was inconsolable and retreated to the apartment, where I told him he could stay until the end of our deal, another two weeks. Elizabeth texted me about a half-hour after our conversation to let me know that Riley's plane was in the air and that our daughter had gone into airplane mode for the moment.

She would try again when the plane gained enough altitude for her to connect to in-flight wi-fi. I thanked her for handling that, knowing that Riley would be hysterical and that I would be blamed. It did not have to be true. If Riley perceived anything to be so, it was true enough.

I longed for a stiff drink. As a Parrot Head, my go-to was a frozen concoction to help me hang on. But this was no mere issue with a heel cut by a pop top. This was death, and I was now haunted by the inescapable images of the *two* corpses I'd all too recently seen—little Imani and the nephew who was like a son to me. What really made me long for the alcohol, though, was realizing what pushed JD over the edge on the very day he thought that his life was coming together, the day he could have sworn he saw the light. Perhaps it's always brightest before the darkness creeps in—or barrels in like a runaway train in the night.

Not wanting to give in to my unhealthy impulses, I poured myself a glass of ice water instead. My head ached from the tragedy and from the previous night of outrunning demons. I should've let them catch me and drag me to a different hell than the real one I was living in. I wanted to feel the pain, all the pain. I *earned* this agony. JD thought he earned the pain, too, but he wouldn't face it. Maybe he also thought I'd be disappointed or furious with him. I was not—well, until after he made that dramatic leap. I know it's cliche for people to express anger when those they love commit suicide, but some cliches exist for good reason.

I turned off the back porch light. It attracted insects, and I felt like sitting in the dark anyway. It's hard to ponder life and death with moths and June bugs pestering you. The realization that JD would never again come from around the corner was crushing my chest like a bag of concrete mix. I just sat. I was in no mood for music—no jazz, no Buffett, no nothing. The cicadas in the pines and frogs in the branch carried on their regular nightly performance as if nothing happened, as if the final collapse of my kingdom was not imminent. To my right I heard the light squeak of a softly opened door. Jack meekly approached.

"I'm sorry," he said.

"I know," I responded without breaking my stare into the darkness ahead that had yet to find any light from a waning crescent moon rising on the other side of the house. "Sit down."

Jack sat in the Adirondack beside me, where JD had plopped down so many times over the previous couple of years, especially on Sundays, when he'd tell his parents he was coming over to take a dip in my pool, though he rarely went for a swim. For a couple of minutes, we just sat still. I sensed he was bracing for another tirade from me.

"*I'm* sorry," I told him as I continued to stare ahead, not wanting to see his sad face. "You were absolutely right."

"I feel like it's my fault," he said. "If I hadn't come down here, none of this would have happened."

"It all still would've happened," I said. "Riley still would have come today. She didn't even know you were here. The only difference is I wouldn't have any idea *why* it happened if you hadn't come. And if I'd have let you say something to him, about being brothers, about being adopted, it could've changed everything. You didn't make this happen. In fact, you were the one person who could have prevented it, and I got in the way. If anybody's at fault, it's me. I was just in disbelief."

"So, you know?"

"I may be a hick, but I ain't stupid, kid. I'm a numbers guy, remember? I can put two and two together, just might take a while—too long in this case. It's just not the kind of thing that would have ever crossed my mind. When did *you* know that JD was the daddy?"

"Panama City," he said. "When he got that call during our trip, he just flipped out, you know."

"I recall."

"I thought he had put it behind him and moved on after falling at the beach," Jack continued. "I think *he* thought he had put it behind him and forgiven himself. I think he assumed Riley was going to, you know, take care of it, even though he didn't like the thought of that, either."

"All that guilt was just too much," I said. "Damn Riley for making a show out of it, coming down here like that. She's never shied away from drama."

"I just can't imagine what he thought when he saw her," Jack said.

"That it was too late, probably," I said. "He still would have been upset, but maybe he could've lived with himself and not—"

I couldn't finish the sentence. In the middle of the backyard, midway between the pool and the railroad tracks, was my favorite tree—a gigantic magnolia that was merely massive when I was a kid. Dad strung a tire swing from it when I was about five. It was the only place Sarah and I really spent time together as children. She would send me flying into space or spinning me into a dizzy stupor. I also spent plenty of summer days sitting alone there, pondering life or bored out of my mind. What I wouldn't have given to feel that carefree daze once again. When I moved Elizabeth and Riley to Possum Holler, one of the first things I did—even before turning the guest house into an art studio for Elizabeth—was to hang a rope swing from that same magnolia's thickest limb that ran horizontal to the ground. It was no tire swing, but it would do, I figured at the time. It was a sturdy, 2x8 piece of pressure-treated yellow pine when I strung it up. Riley, though, rarely used it. Since then, even that pressure-treated wood weathered and withered, and the rope was frayed. Both the swing and the rope taunted me. I vowed to yank them down first thing in the morning—if I mustered the courage to roll out of bed and face real life again.

"What you drinkin'?" Jack asked, interrupting my excruciating stumble down my memory lane that had become overgrown with mental kudzu.

"Water."

"Oh," he said, clearly surprised. "I was a little worried that you might go off the deep end."

"Oh, I'm way off the deep end," I said. "Only a crazy person would be sober right now."

"You know, JD was a little worried about your alcohol use," Jack said warily, obviously hoping I wouldn't snap at him for calling out what any fool could see had become a dependency to cope with the pain of losing Riley to New York and Elizabeth's sugar daddy. I recognized it myself. I just didn't care.

"I don't know why. I was getting pretty good at it." That was as funny as I could be. I'd dropped my old sense of humor somewhere in Querencia Valley while running from the demons. "I'll jump off the wagon again, no doubt about it. Right now, though, I don't know if it makes sense, but I *want* to hurt."

"No, that doesn't make any sense," he said, "but I feel the same way."

"I just feel like he's still here," I said. "I just can't believe he's gone."

"You don't believe in the afterlife at all," Jack asked.

"Not particularly, not in a religious sense, the whole heaven and hell, pearly gates shit," I said. "But I'm not one hundred percent sure about anything. Only idiots are a hundred percent sure about things like that. I don't even know if JD was sure about everything, though he definitely believed most of the Christian stuff—maybe a little too much of it."

"Yeah," Jack mumbled.

"What about you?" I asked earnestly. "JD get you on the team?"

"I had an open mind," he said. "I guess I kind of envied that he had this faith that I didn't. Besides, there've been an awful lot of unexplained coincidences—bumping into Lucas Parsons and those guys last night, you bumping into that girl from decades ago, not to mention my first day here."

"What do you mean?"

"I met JD right here, in this very spot, the first day I got here," he explained. "I didn't rent this place knowing you were his uncle. It was just the closest place I could find to where he lived and went to school. Things just came together weirdly fast."

"So, you're with Jesus now?"

"Not exactly," he said. "Just still open-minded, about everything. I just can't wrap my head around if all this religion stuff is so good, why is there so much bad stuff, too? The age-old question I guess. Especially with someone like JD. Even with you."

"Thanks a lot."

"You know what I mean," he said. "I think you've been through more than you deserve."

"Hell, I might believe in the big guy upstairs more today," I said.

"How so?"

"Maybe he's screwing with us. Maybe it's the Old Testament one—you know, the one who was always testing folks, making bets with the devil, flooding the planet with death, and talking folks into killing their kids, stuff like that. That one. Maybe he is real, and he's got some issues."

"You don't really believe that, do you?"

"Not really. You can't explain everything, and I think that need to explain everything is where religion comes from. And sometimes you climb to the top of Mount Olympus and realize no one was pulling the strings or throwing lightning bolts. And that's when folks realize—well, shit happens."

We sat in silence for the next half-hour. I think we each believed there was nothing further to say that could alleviate our suffering or help us understand JD's drastic action, no matter how much he felt the weight of his perceived sins—ones, it turned out, that were not as grievous as he thought. I stood and patted Jack on the shoulder to reassure him that not only was all well between me and him, but I was grateful for his efforts to pry JD from the cross he bore.

* * *

I don't know how deep into the night Jack stayed out there, but his little red Prius was gone when I peeked out the kitchen window the next morning while brewing a pot of coffee. I did order him to pack his stuff before the incident, so it was plausible that he had quietly removed himself from all the drama. Before I closed the curtain, I saw my sister's familiar white Kia sedan coming up the driveway. This is it, I figured—she's come to kill me. Fair enough. As it drew closer, though, I saw my preacher brother-in-law behind the wheel. I opened the side door to the kitchen and stood there barefoot in my sleep shorts and t-shirt. I greeted him with a simple nod as he stepped out of the car and began walking toward my door.

"Ronnie."

"Ben. Can we talk?"

"Of course," I said. "Coffee will be ready in a minute if you want a cup."

"Hungover?"

I could not tell if he was truly concerned about my drinking the way JD was or was trying to lash out, something that did not fit with his usual measured demeanor.

"Actually, I quit drinking," I said.

"When?"

"Friday." Ronnie looked off to the side as if there were an invisible person to get his "Can you believe this guy?" glance.

"Visitation is tomorrow afternoon, and the funeral's Wednesday morning," he said. I nodded and stirred a teaspoon of sugar into my cup. "I'd rather you not come. Your young friend, either."

"If that's what you want," I agreed. Neither was an event I *wanted* to attend. It wasn't like JD would be there, just a bunch of side-eyed, judgmental church folks.

"Sarah doesn't want you there," he said. I said nothing, just shrugged my shoulders. "Where's your young friend, Jack?"

"Not sure, to be honest," I admitted. "He's taking all this harder than you might expect."

"Well, they *are* brothers," Ronnie said matter-of-factly.

"What the hell?"

"I didn't catch it at the hospital that day," he said. "I was focused on other things, as you can imagine. But when y'all came to dinner that night after the tornado, I knew. It's a powerful feeling when you see your own eyes in another human being."

"I'm sorry," I stammered. "Look, I know they're brothers. Jack told me—just yesterday, in fact. But I also know JD was adopted."

"They're *both* my sons, Ben—my real, biological sons," he said. I rubbed my hands through my thinning hair and shook my head.

"But—"

"Sarah doesn't know," he said, "and I'd appreciate it if we could keep it that way. At least for now."

"Jesus, Ronnie, I'm more confused than I was yesterday."

"Did Jack say anything to JD about them being brothers?" he asked as he looked me dead in the eyes. "Is that why—"

"No," I interrupted. "He was going to, and I wish he had. I stopped him—another screw-up on my part. This doesn't make any sense, Ronnie."

He explained that he played guitar in a rock band throughout the nineties, though they never made a name for themselves outside of the Northeast and New York City. My sister had taken a liking to them and followed them from show to show. However, he was in a relationship at the time with one of the lead singers, a girl named Natalie. The name sounded familiar, but I couldn't place it. He gave up Natalie for my sister and found Jesus about the same time. He tried to reinvent his musical career as a contemporary Christian artist but found little interest in the Northeast, so he decided instead to pursue preaching. He didn't go to seminary and instead studied at what he called a "Bible institute." He and Sarah immediately got married so that they wouldn't be living in sin. However, a couple of months into the marriage, he got a call from Natalie's sister telling him that she had been killed in a car wreck in California. She had other news, too. Natalie had given birth to twin boys just a couple months before the accident and abandoned them at a fire station in Pawtucket, Rhode Island, under a safe haven law. Natalie had told her that Ronnie was the father.

He couldn't handle the guilt, he said, but didn't have the courage to tell Sarah the truth. He quietly visited the orphanage only to find out one of the boys was still in the hospital, while the other had been adopted by a family that had been longing for a child of their own for years. He then made up some bullshit story about the Lord laying it upon his heart to visit the sick child in the hospital, where he found out the baby was being treated for meningitis. He told Sarah the Lord spoke to him at the hospital, reminding him about how the baby Moses was shipped down the river. He said the Lord wanted them to care for this "orphaned" baby, that the Lord had special plans for him. They prayed together for the baby's recovery. Then they prayed for guidance. They held hands as they prayed for direction, and his hands began to shake — moved by his lies more than divine intervention, I imagine. Sarah told him she felt *something*. Then and there, they decided that they would work to adopt JD. He said he knew that he could never have convinced her to take on two babies, not that it was even possible with Jack having already found a comfortable home with well-to-do parents. As soon as JD's adoption was finalized, well after he was released from the hospital, they moved to

Possum Holler with my parents while Ronnie pursued more Bible studies in the South.

"So, Sarah doesn't know you're JD's biological father? Damn, Ronnie!"

"And she doesn't know about Jack, either," he said. "I thought Jack may have told him, and that sent over the edge."

"Well, don't worry," I said sternly. "You haven't been outed."

"Ben, I promise I will tell her about Jack, someday, when the time is right," he insisted. "But not right now. She can't handle it."

"Uh-huh." I didn't believe him for a second.

"I need your word that you won't say anything," he said with his lips quivering. "I love Sarah. You know that."

"I don't know nothin' 'bout nothin' right now, Ronnie—except that the best time for the truth to come out would have been yesterday! All these damn lies! And you call yourself a fucking preacher!"

"Ben—"

"Just leave, Ronnie! I won't go to the funeral, and if I see Jack—you know, your *son*—I'll make sure he doesn't go, either! And I won't say anything to Sarah. It's not like we're close. But all these lies are gonna burn you up, man. Look, I could not be more sorry about JD. It's literally killing me. But I thought *my* life was fucked up, and it damn sure is. But you've got issues."

"I'm not disputing that," he said.

"Good to see you're honest about something," I said as I stood and opened the door for him to leave. He somberly obliged.

I thought of all the times Ronnie had looked down upon me with judgment, as if he had the moral high ground because he believed all those Bible stories—or supposedly did. He was breaking one of the most basic Commandments that his folks were so keen on posting everywhere. It was more than just bearing false witness, I thought—he's a goddamn liar. He was one of the most respected people in the community, a man of the cloth, even though he had never actually attended seminary. (Rural Southern churches are not always sticklers for certifications—you just have to "hear the call" or need a get-out-of-Hell-free card.) For all of the scorn I'd received from family, Muckalee Christian, and most of the local community, and despite the litany of well-intended mistakes I'd made, I came to a realization at that moment, one that had never crossed my mind:

I was the most honest man in Possum Holler.

The only person I lied to...was myself. As my way-too-open and talkative Wall Street colleague Josh once told me, "I've found it easier to tell the embarrassing truth than it is to keep up with my lies." Of course, that was after he handed me a card for his favorite rub-and-tug masseuse in The Big Apple.

* * *

The temperature in Possum Holler hit triple digits that afternoon. It was enough to, well, make an opossum holler. Not me, though—I was too drunk to raise my voice. I lay back on the steps of my pool with my right arm resting on the concrete deck within easy reach of a fifth of tequila that rested in a bucket of ice. It didn't get to rest for extended periods as I kept grabbing it for another swig. I had two days of miserable soberness to make up for. I couldn't bear the blender's skull-rattling grind required for that frozen concoction that once helped me hang on. The air was sticky and stagnant yet again, and the breeze alternated between one and zero miles per hour. It was perfectly miserable —and fitting.

I heard a vehicle pull up near the side of the house and then the slamming of a door. My brain anticipated it was JD, but then I remembered it was not Sunday. And, oh yeah, JD was gone. Perhaps it was Sarah coming to reiterate how much she did not want me at the funeral in two days. Then again, it could be Ronnie dropping by with a shotgun to make sure I kept his lies intact. Whatever. I took another swig of tequila and lay my head back against the edge of the top step so the sun could continue frying what remained of my brain. I was stirred from my zombie state by the smell of Samburgers.

"You need to eat," Jack said as stepped onto my back deck and plopped down a grease-soaked brown paper bag. "Got you three double-chili-cheese *without*, fries, and a Diet Coke. That's your usual, ain't it?"

"What if I'm not hungry?"

"What's that gotta do with eating Samburgers?" he asked. "Besides, no more half-assed heart attacks. Let's do it right next time."

"Jesus, what got into you?" I asked as I lifted my waterlogged and tequila-logged body out of the water and stumbled over to the Adirondack chairs.

"I'm just glad you're wearing a swimsuit," he said. "Formal occasion?"

"I've already had one visitor today," I said. "Figured everybody's distraught enough. How you doin'?"

"Just trying to figure out what I'm supposed to be feeling right now," he said. "Sadness? Anger? Confusion? All of the above? I feel like I had this connection, you know, like a gap in my life was filled. And just like that it was ripped wide open again."

I unwrapped one of the burgers. Those wonderfully greasy little sliders came in buns that were paired, so they would break the buns in two when someone, as I always did, ordered them in an odd number. I always started with the lonely double-chili-cheese first. I ran my finger along the side and scooped up some of the chili that had tried to escape. Then I lifted the top of the bun for inspection.

"Looking for something?" Jack asked.

"The meaning of life," I said.

"Let me know if you find it, please."

"Actually, I'm looking for onions—well, *one* onion. Sometimes they get going pretty quick on the grill back there and one of those little yellow onions gets separated from the group or defects to the *without* tribe. Or maybe they're just fucking with me because they like to see me wince when I bite into one of those radioactive little boogers."

"I doubt they know me, so they're probably not fucking with you today."

"Ha," I said as I thumped the underside of the top bun. "A stowaway. Apparently they don't like you, either. You didn't get anything?"

"Actually, I got a chili dog *all the way* and a double cheeseburger *all the way*," he said.

"All the way? With onions? Who are you? Ugh. And who gets one Samburger? That's like going to KFC and asking for a one-piece bucket."

"You know, your whole heart attack thing is starting to make sense now," he said. "I thought you were a little young for a brush with death."

"Yeah, but what I lack in age I make up for with poor judgment."

"I got it to go, though," he said. "Your idea of ambiance and mine may be a little different."

"Well, your car's gonna smell like Samburgers all the way back to Boston," I said.

"Cool," he said with a half smile that seemed wistful even though he had a few more days before he was to head back to Boston. "Actually, I went down to the river and ate."

"The Thinking Spot?"

"Yeah."

"There's no crime scene tape? And how'd you get down there anyway yesterday? I thought there were all kinds of trees and limbs and stuff down after the tornado."

"JD—" He paused to collect himself. "He had cleared out just enough to get his truck down there. Guess it was real important to him. And, no. No crime tape. No nothing. It was like nothing happened. It was just...very quiet."

"By the way," I said as I crumpled the greasy burger wrapper and shoved it into the bag while also retrieving the remaining two burgers, "Ronnie dropped by."

"JD's dad?"

"Uh, yeah. My sister doesn't want me—or you—at the funeral, or the visitation."

"What?"

"Sorry," I said. "I'm sure it's all about me and nothing to do with you, kid. She no doubt blames me—and Riley—for everything. She's probably right. I wish Riley had nothing to do with it. Now, I've got broken heart syndrome *and* I'm pissed."

"I guess funerals are really only for the people left behind anyway," Jack said.

"I don't know why folks have 'em," I said. "I mean, if the deceased could sit up and thank everyone for coming at the end, maybe. But they're just excruciating. Hell, I've been to two of 'em this summer, and I don't know if I could take another. That one for little Imani, Travis' granddaughter—damn, that was rough. Black folks, in the South anyway, tend to be more emotional in church anyway, whether they're happy or grieving. And they love worshipping...for *hours*."

"What about Southern white folks?"

"More boring, quietly excruciating. Although, this one may be a bit crazier. Everybody loved JD. He's about the only kid at school who fit in with any group he wanted—the jocks, the nerds, the Jesus freaks, the rednecks, you name it. It was only the racist kids he apparently had any issues with, and he kept that to himself. Well, until that ballgame anyway."

"Been to any white people's funerals lately?" he asked as if he were actually doing research about the South for a sociology project or something. I sensed we were coming full-circle.

"No, but I approved of some."

"Ah, the old Mark Twain line."

"You're smarter than you look," I said. "Last one I went to was ten years ago, after my dad died just two months after my mom died. We hadn't been close since I left for college and New York, even though he's the one who pushed me to pursue an Ivy League education. I wasn't exactly ambitious then and would have been OK with a Kudzu League education. Of course, later he thought my Yankee days changed me and that I didn't appreciate home as much as I should have. I guess once you immerse yourself in a new world for long enough, it rubs off on you a little. Anyway, it was rough. Dad died a few days after his birthday. I'd been so wrapped up in work and stuff that I had totally forgotten his birthday—no card, no phone call, nothing. Needless to say, that didn't exactly help my bad relationship with Sarah. Probably had something to do with why I came home after he left us all of this," I said with an arm gesture toward the house and then to the back yard. "I guess I felt like I owed something to my dad. That's when I made the dumb decision to buy out Sarah and bring Riley and Elizabeth down here."

"I'm not sure it was dumb," Jack said. "This is an incredible place. You can't blame Possum Holler for everything."

"Riley and Elizabeth can—well, after blaming me first. It's all muddy water under the bridge now. Speaking of which, you know that little foot bridge over Boggy Branch down there near the tracks?"

"Yeah."

"That was where I wanted my 'funeral'," I said while making the air quotes with my greasy fingers. "I didn't want to be buried in a cemetery with all these neighbors. I'm claustrophobic anyway. I wanted to be cremated and then have my ashes dropped off that bridge into the branch, float down to Timber Creek, hit the Flint River, drift on down to the Apalachicola and into the Gulf of Mexico and then...who knows? Of course, the way everything has gone downhill, I would have probably gotten stuck in some slough and swallowed by a bullfrog anyway."

"You got a new plan?" he asked.

"Why? You know something I don't?"

"Well, you are wolfing those burgers down pretty hard, not to mention you're drunk at two in the afternoon."

"I was sober for two days, and I don't know whether you noticed or not, but those days kinda sucked," I said. "But no, don't dump me in the branch, please."

"Why not?"

"Because it ain't gonna be my bridge much longer," I told him matter-of-factly. I thought it might hurt to say it aloud, but all I felt was relief, mixed with a tinge of heartburn.

"What do you mean?"

"I'm selling the place—the house, the land, the whole kingdom. I'm abdicating. You want it?"

"I'm sorry, what? When did you decide this?"

"A half-hour ago."

"*After* you got drunk?"

"I haven't made a smart sober decision in over a decade, kid," I said.

"You'll reconsider when the tequila wears off by tomorrow."

"Nope," I insisted. "Besides, I don't plan on sobering up for a while. I tried embracing the pain and drowning the pain, and I prefer the latter. Seriously, I've considered it a few times over the past couple of years, ever since Riley left. But I felt like I owed something to the kids at school when I was a teacher. And I was the one person JD felt like he could talk honestly to—though, clearly, he didn't tell me everything. But, now, I got nothin' tying me to this place, or to Possum Holler. Nothin' but pain. I'm ready to go hurt somewhere else, somewhere new."

"It's your call," he admitted. "I just think this is a great place. Plus, it's family land. I'd kill to have a family place. OK, that's a poor choice of words. You know what I mean."

"You've got family, kid, and you've got a place," I said as I looked him in the eyes, where Ronnie's genes were now impossible to *not* see. I wanted to tell him more. After all, I was the most honest man in Possum Holler. It wasn't my lie to hide, but it wasn't my truth to share, either. If he had known what to ask, I'd have given him the honest answer. But Jack didn't come to Possum Holler looking for his father. He came to find his brother.

"True."

"They *wanted* you. They *chose* you. There's something to be said for that. The little bit of family I do have left, they don't give a crap about me. Hell, I *barely* give a crap about me."

"Not that it's the same, but I give a crap," he said. "You're my brother's uncle. Given the circumstances, I'm gonna call it family."

"I don't have it in me to be *your* crazy uncle," I told him. "But I appreciate the sentiment. I'm sorry your so-called 'sociology project' blew up."

"I found what I was looking for," he said as he looked toward the ground, "and lost it just as fast. I thought things were supposed to move slower here. I thought you said nothing ever happened in Possum Holler."

"Nothing did until *you* showed up. Not that it's your fault, mind you, but I blame you anyway," I said with what almost qualified as a grin.

"Even though it's not my fault, huh?"

"Exactly. It's family tradition to blame someone else for anything that goes awry."

# Yonder Way

After the funeral service, the family—*invited* family anyway—was to gather briefly at the graveside for some quick words and prayer before he was lowered into the rust-colored dirt in the tiny cemetery near Riverside Free Will. Because the church was even younger than JD, he would have only a handful of neighbors. When he was lowered, the average age of the cemetery residents likely dropped to about sixty. I believe he would have preferred to have had his ashes spread into the water at his Thinking Spot, rather than spend eternity hanging with those old ghosts, but I was not consulted, and teenagers don't exactly make their final wishes known.

At my urging, Jack agreed to stay through Saturday, which was supposed to be his final day in the apartment all along. The Yankee stranger who'd rolled into Possum Holler six weeks earlier was the closest thing I had to a family member or anyone who gave a crap. Besides, a deal is a deal, and I was, again, the most honest man in Possum Holler. Of course, that unofficial title would soon be up for grabs.

As JD's other family mourned with friends and fellow church members, I made coffee and toast and checked my finances. For all of my personal failings, I was damn good at turning some money into a lot of money. I'd taken the savings from my Wall Street days and my substantial Bitcoin profits that had begun almost as a joke and turned it into quite the nest egg by investing half in steady-growth mutual funds while using the other half as the power supply for my online stock trading. I had more than tripled the value of those funds since leaving New York by simply relying on my proven cynicism instead of the Wall Street media experts' constantly fluctuating tips. While most day-traders seemed to chase the next big thing in technology, finance or health care, I bought stock in boring, well-established companies. Every time market reports used words like *spooked*, *panic*, *worried*, *frightened*, or anything of the sort, I sank money into it. It doesn't take a genius to look at a chart of the past year, or two, or ten, or one hundred to understand that every blip and every crash is temporary. It ultimately creeps upward forever. You just have to be willing to ride out the storms. Strangely enough, it was always the financial geniuses the reports cited as being spooked, panicked, or worried. I was a *yeah whatever* investor. Besides, I had history classes to teach back then and didn't have time to make money by buying or selling one hour and doing the opposite the next hour. I didn't *enjoy* trading—I merely *understood* it. It's not rocket science. Any idiot with a little bit of capital can do it.

But this idiot wanted a break from that, too. Besides, I needed to free up cash for where I was heading. I didn't know where that might be, but I was sure wherever I wound up they'd be happy to take my money. My tastes were cheap, though, and I knew that no matter where I landed, my funds would long outlive me and be available for Riley's ambiguous future—and perhaps set up a grandchild for the future, as well. I spent the morning cashing out half of my investments. Tequila wasn't the only liquid asset I needed. Of course, if I were still advising others on their investments, I'd definitely encourage them to buy tequila stocks or agave futures given my state of mind.

I closed the laptop but had more business ahead. I may have been drunk when I finalized my long-flirted-with decision to sell the kingdom, but it made even more sense in the sobering light of a new day. I had the financial means to leave, and there was nothing holding me back. I was free to waste my life away where there wasn't a memory haunting me around every corner. I could make new haunting memories somewhere else—and, with any luck, drink them away day after day until those memories were gone with the wind—or *Gone with the Fried Green Crawdads*.

Speaking of remembering nothing, an unopened white envelope caught my eye. The letter Shantae had delivered a few days earlier lay on the kitchen counter teasing me. It had not slipped my mind, but it felt inappropriate to open it while we were grieving the loss of JD. That encounter with Jenny Jacobs, the girl who gave me my first kiss thirty-five years ago, as well as my most recent one, reminded me too much of the day JD snapped at the beach and fell from the balcony. My curiosity, however, couldn't be held at bay any longer.

* * *

*Dear Ben,*

*I just wanted to apologize for dragging you into my drama. It was just such a crazy coincidence, or supernatural intervention, that we bumped into each other at the beach. I don't know what the universe is trying to tell us, but I don't want to lose touch. I looked for you on Facebook but didn't see you. I hope you don't mind that I sent this to your school, but it was the only way I could find you. Anyway, my divorce will be final any day, in case you're wondering. And we could all use a new friend—even if it's an old new friend. (Well, not that old!) Here's my contact info if you're ever this way again. It was good seeing you.*

*Phinz up,*

*Jenny*

* * *

Wow. She actually cited the mysterious universe instead of Jesus Christ for throwing us together. It was a rare sign of hope. Even the wildest girls from my teenage years had become faithful church ladies by this point, yet Jenny didn't appear compelled to credit God for our random-as-hell meeting, or to bless me, or to pray for me, or anything churchy. Could it be that she was an abnormal freak like me? It was so refreshing that I decided to keep the letter. I didn't intend to contact her anytime soon, and I damn sure wasn't getting on Facebook again, but she was right: You never know when you might need a friend. For the moment, though, I was content to hang out with my buddies Monte Alban and Jose Cuervo. I placed the letter under my truck keys, next to the note Lucas Parsons had left for Jack, before heading to my bathroom for a shower. Monte and Jose would have to wait. I had important business that afternoon in Montezuma, and it had nothing to do with Samburgers...for a change.

* * *

The old bell on the glass door to Flint Realty jingled behind me as if to cue some Monty Python skit. But I wasn't there with an ex-parrot—just a dead dream.

"May I help—oh, hi there, Ben. What can I do for you?"

"I'm moving."

"What? Where?"

"Somewhere else. Ain't looking to buy, just to sell."

Alyssa Anderson and I were the same age. While she grew up in Montezuma, she had attended Muckalee Christian since eighth grade, while I stayed in the Macon County public schools. My folks could have scraped up the money to send me to private school back then, but I knew I wouldn't fit in with the Alyssa crowd who rode a private bus twenty miles from Montezuma to Americus until they had friends old enough to drive and carpool. Of course, I didn't fit in as a teacher there, either. The headmaster was right—I really wasn't Muckalee material. Being educated in the public school system was probably for the best, though. Had I dived into a "Christian" educational environment at the same time I was beginning my escape from organized religion, it might have driven me crazy much earlier in life. I would have been as wild as my sister as a teen and would have never gone off to Brown, built a successful career, and formed a perfect family to destroy. However, it's doubtful I'd have wound up marrying a preacher like Sarah did.

"I'm real sorry about JD," Alyssa said. "And I hate we didn't have a chance to speak at the funeral. I didn't even see you. Of course, it was a huge crowd. So sad."

"Yeah."

She knew damn well I wasn't there. Alyssa was friends with my sis through their Garden Club. She wouldn't be caught dead attending Riverside Free Will Church, though. She was a proper Southern Baptist, the kind that disliked Jesus' teachings even more than the folks at Free Will. Her crowd was the type to feel oppressed because they couldn't express their hate as freely as they could decades earlier. I didn't have to like her for this visit, though. I knew she could turn on her country club charm and sell the old home place as quickly as any human could move a Possum Holler property—not that I expected a sale anytime soon. I was unaware of anyone recently selling so much as a trailer or an acre of land anywhere near Possum Holler. I'd calculated my kingdom was worth at least $600,000, but I wasn't exactly digging in my heels. I wasn't desperate for cash. I wanted to wash my hands of it.

Alyssa insisted it had to be worth more than $750,000. I signed the papers for her to list it. I didn't need to go agent shopping in Montezuma, Georgia. Besides, she could easily bat her eyelashes and shake her ass for an extra ten percent. As I stood to leave, I reiterated that I just wanted to be done with the place.

"Alyssa, you could sell it for a damn dollar, and I'd probably agree. What's six percent of a buck anyway?"

"Um, six cents."

"Well, they don't make pennies anymore, so make it a dime. I'm feeling generous."

"Actually, Ben, I think $750,000 is quite reasonable, especially with all of these rich hunters coming up from Florida looking for play-around land."

"Fine with me," I said as I slapped my palms against my knees and stood to leave. "Seriously, Alyssa, just sell the goddamn property!" After shutting the door, I felt bad for leaving in a huff. I paused on the sidewalk and peeked my head back inside the office. "I'm sorry, Alyssa. I meant *please* sell the goddamn property."

"Well, will do," she replied meekly with her fake smile before most certainly unleashing a torrent of harsh words for me as soon as I re-closed the door.

* * *

I spent the next two days packing what little I would need for my trip to—wherever the hell I was headed. I stayed sober because I knew that packing with a headache would be a real bitch. Besides, I wanted my next drink to be at *my* church—the beach, where I would confess all my sins and beg for forgiveness from Mother Ocean. And if she would show me the light, I'd be happy to put the bottle down. Upon which beaches I would worship, however, I had no idea. Just thinking of Panama City made my face hurt. I wanted to hit a few coastal communities I'd never heard of. I didn't want to follow the well-trodden tourist paths in the shadows of overpriced condos. I longed to explore some communities of misfits and characters instead of conformists. My plan, if you could call it that, was to head down the east coast of Florida, all the way to the Southernmost Point in Key West, and then make my way back up the Gulf side. By then, maybe I'd have an idea which sandy *church* I wanted to join. If not, there was always the Georgia coast—which is rich in history with much of its environment protected and islands not overrun by high-rises and tacky attractions. I wasn't quirky enough for Savannah, nor wealthy enough for Saint Simons, but maybe there was some fishing village where legends like Blackbeard bopped around back in the day. After years in New York, the only thing I was certain of was that the Outer Banks would be the northernmost limit of my exploration. If I hadn't discovered a fitting hideaway by that point, then I'd just settle for the prototypical retreat to Key West with the other freaks and Buffett wannabes.

I crammed two suitcases full of comfortable summer attire. I intended to take little else besides my laptop and guitar. My driving finger was getting more flexible, almost enough to strum again. As for everything else, I planned to return to Possum Holler only after the property was under contract and probably offer most of the furniture to some local charity or shelter. They could use it, sell it, or burn it for heat next winter. I didn't care.

I reserved no hotel rooms in advance. I didn't want to commit to any location. When Sarah and I were young, Dad would start our summer vacations by carrying our limp, sleepy bodies to the car about four in the morning and driving south to avoid traffic. We'd wake up in Florida, usually Panama City, Daytona or Pensacola, and I'd be sent into the lobbies of various cheap hotels to ask if they had any rooms available and how much. Then we'd pile into some beachfront room that reeked of cigarettes with burn holes in the comforters. If it was good enough for him, it was good enough for me—well, except for the ash-heavy rooms that were mostly a thing of the past. I tossed my tent and sleeping bag into the back of the truck just in case Dad's old plan wasn't foolproof.

By Friday morning, I was antsy. I mopped, vacuumed, and straightened up the house. I never knew what Mama meant when she told us to "straighten up" our rooms as kids. I suspect it was her polite way of telling us to get shit off the floors and out of her damn way. I wasn't on a quest to get the place ready for a *Southern Living* magazine profile, but maybe they could feature it in their "Good Enough" issue.

I went into Montezuma for lunch and settled into my usual booth at Sam's Snack Shack with a special order for a change: *two* chili-cheeseburgers *without*, a chili dog *without*, fries, and a Diet Coke. I knew it might be the last time to experience the culinary delights and ambiance of my favorite greasy spoon, so I added a hot dog to balance out the burgers. I was savoring my last French fry when I felt a hand on my shoulder.

"Hey, young man!"

"Hey, Henry! Have a seat."

"Lemme hold two dollars," he said.

"What? You done spent all your pension from the Spanish-American War?"

"Naw, I left my wallet at home. I need a couple of thighs."

"Don't we all, brother?" I dug out my wallet. "Here."

"Damn," he said as I handed him a twenty. "Who's this fella again?"

"Andrew Jackson."

"Oh, yeah. I remember him. Good man."

"He was an *awful* person," I said.

"That's what I said. I'll bring your change."

"Keep it, Henry." I didn't know Henry's real story, nor how old he really was. Having been pretty good with numbers my whole life, I suspected his report of being 126 years old might have been off by a few decades. I just knew that he was a decent man with an uncanny knack for detecting inclement weather with his leg. That alone deserved respect. "It was good to see you, sir."

After finishing my final Samburger I weaved my way through the crowd of hungry customers between the ordering counter and front door and stood for a moment on the sidewalk to look each way and take a mental snapshot. I peered through the large glass window between the flyers for church revivals and items for sale and saw Henry returning to his seat with a bag of chicken and a Coke. He flashed that snaggletoothed smile and waved with appreciation. I gave him a quick salute and grinned—albeit mildly—for the first time in days. I doubted I'd see the old man again. Folks rarely make it to 127, especially those who like their chicken fried. I dropped by the Piggly Wiggly on the way home and picked up a couple of bone-in ribeyes and potatoes to bake. I sent Jack a text and told him to join me for one last tasty dinner. The kid deserved a decent sendoff. Instead of drowning our pain, I suggested we devour it instead with a night of grilling on the deck. Before I bid farewell to the house and to Jack, though, I had one more goodbye on the agenda.

I drove slowly past my sister's house to see if their car was there. It wasn't. Still, I quietly eased into the nearby church's parking lot and stopped between the sanctuary and the little cemetery. The dirt around JD's grave was fresh. I didn't talk to the ground as many are inclined to do. If we do have a soul, neither a casket nor six feet of dirt would be able to confine it. Someday a scientist will figure out exactly what happens when we die, and all the preachers of the world will have to find new jobs. I could be wrong, and I'll repent as fast as possible if Jesus does descend from the heavens. Hopefully, he will be on the side of the folks like me who agree with him instead of the ones who supposedly love him but aren't too keen on what he supposedly taught.

The thought of JD's body already deteriorating underneath made me uneasy. I reminded myself that I'd better make official my wishes to be cremated—*after* I'm dead, of course, as much as some folks in Possum Holler would gladly chase me down with pitchforks and torches to cremate me alive. Then again, to whom would I even convey such wishes?

As I walked back toward the truck, I noticed the front door to the church slightly ajar. The last place I felt like being was inside ol' Riverside Free Pass Church, but I also didn't want anybody entering the place and stealing—well, whatever you can steal from a church. Bibles, choir robes, holy water, stale crackers, souls? I don't know. I poked my head inside and saw Sis sitting in a pew, alone, three rows from the back. I crept into the chapel and took a seat in the very back row. She continued staring blankly ahead.

"You smell like a Samburger," she said softly without turning to acknowledge me.

"Um, you're welcome."

"Why are you here? This is not exactly your kind of place."

"I just dropped by for a minute. Sis, I am so sorry." She didn't respond. "By the way, I'm leaving."

"Good. When?"

"Tomorrow," I said. "I'm selling everything—the house, the land. Alyssa's gonna handle everything. Of course, if you and Ronnie—"

"No thank you."

"Did something happen there when we were kids that I don't know about?" I asked, genuinely not understanding why the thought of that place disgusted her so.

"No. We had the perfect small-town life, wonderful parents. You were their little angel, and I was the problem first-born."

"If they could see us now," I said.

"Ben, do you know when I became a Christian—I mean seriously?"

"When Ronnie found Jesus and y'all got married?"

"I never told you this, but it doesn't matter now: JD was adopted." I faked a surprised expression just in case she turned around. She didn't. "He was in the hospital with meningitis, this poor little angel who had been abandoned by his mother, left at a fire station. Ronnie had just really started studying the Bible intensely, and when he found out about this child, he visited the hospital and felt the Lord calling us to raise him. We prayed about it. We asked the Lord to heal him, and in a few weeks, he improved. Other than a little bit of hearing loss, he was just fine. It was the first miracle I've witnessed."

I wanted to ask her how that "God is good all the time" thing was working out. I longed to tell her that the whole foundation for adopting JD was based upon huge lies by her beloved husband and that she would not have to go very far to find JD's biological father. But, again, it wasn't my lie to hide nor my truth to tell.

"Again, I'm sorry, but you're not the only one who's heartbroken," I told her. She shook her head in disbelief that I'd act as if I understood her pain. "Well, I'll leave you alone. Goodbye, Sis."

She ignored me. It was understandable. She hated me long before that summer. I was getting used to it. The only family who cared about me at all was JD, and it turned out he was no more family to me than Jack was—biologically speaking anyway. I quietly walked out of Riverside Free Pass Church for the final time but didn't leave the door ajar as I had found it. I softly closed it completely, turning the handle so slowly that Sarah couldn't hear the click as it shut.

As my truck neared the driveway to my soon-to-be former house, I was greeted by Alyssa Anderson's sickeningly beautiful smile adorning a Flint Realty sign near the mailbox. "Damn, girl don't waste no time," I muttered aloud. "That sign might work if anybody ever drove by here."

Later, Jack gathered a few broken limbs from around my dying kingdom while I grilled dinner. We dined at my small wrought-iron table on the deck as a warm breeze swept the backyard. I lit the wood Jack had placed in my firepit and retrieved our dessert—marshmallows to roast on the ends of a couple of sweetgum switches I'd sharpened with my pocket knife. Jack excused himself to go into the apartment and returned with a couple of watermelon-flavored High Noons.

"Wow," I said. "I apologize for thinking you were a little girly before. You're actually a *lot* girly."

"They were JD's," he said. "They're leftover from our camping trip that didn't quite happen as planned."

"Well, I wasn't going to drink anything at least until I got to St. Somewhere or wherever I'm going, but I doubt these count as drinking," I said as I stood to take mine and popped the top.

"Hang on," Jack said as he poured a little from his can into the fire, which sizzled upon contact. "To my brother."

I smiled and followed suit. "To JD."

Jack streamed JD's favorite Brasstown Baldies songs from his phone, and we had our own damn funeral for JD, a proper one. I shared as many stories about his JD as Jack could pack into his memory for the ride home. We laughed wistfully but shed no tears. As the flames turned the embers and the skeeters came to call, Jack stood from his Adirondack chair with a look of resignation. His mission wasn't just complete—it was over. I don't think he was ready to go home, but he knew it was time. So did I.

"I'll see you in the morning," he said as he extended his hand for a shake as I stood up with him. I grabbed his hand and pulled him in for a hug. I could hear him sniffle.

"Oh, cut it out, kid. I do this for all my guests."

"I thought I was your only guest."

"What's your point? Now go to bed. You've got a long drive ahead of you."

Jack opened the door to the apartment but before entering, he turned and said, "Goodnight, Uncle Ben."

"You know I hate that," I said as I looked toward the night sky with fake exasperation and a touch of wistfulness as I knew it might be the last time I ever heard that moniker. "Night, kid."

I sat back down and watched the embers fade until the tiniest speck of orange remained. With no fuel for that spark, the fire would soon be history. I didn't want to see the once-roaring blaze reduced to smoke and then cold ashes, so I gave up on the evening and went to bed myself. That night I dreamed of Riley and woke myself up crying as I had done dozens of times over the past couple of years. I always tried to avoid thinking of Riley before falling asleep for fear it would spark one of those painful dreams. It didn't matter what was happening between me and Riley in those dreams, good or bad. Somehow, I'd still wake up in tears. As painful as my final night in the house was, though, it was fitting. I couldn't wait for morning. I was sad to leave and, yet, eager to go. I was ready to leave *all* my dreams behind, including the tear-jerking ones.

* * *

The truck was packed. I surveyed the kitchen a final time to make sure I was leaving nothing behind. I grabbed the letter from Jenny Jacobs and the note from Lucas Parsons but nothing else. I locked the door to the house for the final time as Jack was slamming the lid to his packed trunk.

"Where ya headed?" he asked as he fiddled with his key fob.

"Yonder way, I reckon," I said as I motioned southward with the letter still in my hand.

"I mean, you got a plan? What's the destination?"

"God only knows," I said while not breaking eye contact with the road south.

"So, that means—"

"*No one* knows. Hell if *I* know. The planned life can only be endured, kid—and I don't think I can endure one more goddamn thing."

"Please tell me you're not doing some kind of 'Leaving Las Vegas' thing," he said as he grabbed my arm. "I'm serious."

"More of a 'Leaving Possum Holler' thing. No, kid, I ain't gonna kill myself or drink myself to death, if that's what you mean—at least not on purpose. I just might have a grandchild on the way, I think. I may never meet 'em, but that's the last grain of hope on the sands of the desolate beach that's my life now. Maybe it's time to go back to *my* church and repent."

"Heading for the coast, huh?"

"Yep. Probably some little beach town where nobody knows me and nobody cares. Or a beach shack in the middle of nowhere. Or every bar with a view between here and the Keys. Folks around here have been telling me to get lost for years. I may be a little slow, but I think I'm gonna finally take their advice."

"Send me an email when you get there?" he asked as he extended his hand for a final handshake.

"I doubt it," I said while lightly gripping his hand. I was done with vigorously engaging other humans. "Oh, take this."

I handed him the note from Lucas Parsons.

"What's this?" he asked.

"From the Brasstown Baldies fella," I said with a smile. "Maybe he thinks you've got some talent or something. I mean, I think you suck."

"Badge of honor," he replied.

"Can I give you a little advice?"

"Sure."

"You're a good listener," I told him as I let go and looked back to the highway. "At some point, I quit listening to everyone, to the world—and, lo and behold, the world quit talking to me. Keep listening. The only thing lonelier than having no one to talk to is having no one—and *nothing*—to hear. The world gets mighty quiet."

"I thought you said that was a good thing."

"If you *choose* it, yeah," I said as I turned back to look him in the eyes. "But when the quiet chooses *you*, not so much."

Jack nodded.

"I guess I had some hopes that were a little idealistic about coming here, meeting my brother, and maybe even learning a little more about myself," he said. "Turns out, I'm as confused as ever."

"I know the feeling," I said with a grimace. "Don't give up hope, kid. You've got plenty of time. Hell, I wouldn't be surprised to see you touring with the Brasstown Baldies someday. Whatever you do, wherever you go, enjoy the ride. Don't dig in your heels anywhere. The world's a helluva lot bigger than Possum Holler—bigger than Boston for that matter."

I knew he was not ready to let go of his kinda sorta family, but the previous night he received the last hug I had in me. I patted him awkwardly on his shoulder.

"Still not the huggy-feely type, huh," he noted as he wiped away a tear.

He tossed the still-folded note into the passenger seat, and plopped down behind the wheel with his hands placed properly at ten and two as he stared ahead with no expression. Finally, he dipped his head for a moment in resignation and nodded as if his internal dialogue agreed that the time had come.

"Hey!" I yelled after he started the engine. He let down the driver's side window. "If you do write that *Gone with the Fried Green Crawdads* book, send me a copy. Come up with a better ending, though. The current one sucks."

"Hey, Ben," he said as I turned away.

"Yeah."

"I gotta tell you something before I go."

"Oh crap. I'm gonna need a drink, ain't I?"

"Actually, no. Do you know why JD came over here so much on Sundays to hang out?"

"I'm fairly certain it was to steal pearls of wisdom from the King of Possum Holler," I said. "But I take it you think differently."

"He did it for Riley," he said. "She was worried about you. He was keeping an eye on you...for her."

"Is that what he told you?"

"Not in as many words," he admitted. "Call it a sixth sense."

"You're not going to tell me you're a ghost, are you?" I asked facetiously. "Wait, am *I* a ghost?"

"You been shot lately?"

"This kid Stevie shot me with a BB gun in fifth grade," I said.

"You need better friends," he said. "Seriously, Riley still loves you."

"I appreciate you trying to make me feel better, but, no. You haven't seen the way she lashes out at me."

"People don't lash out at people they don't care about," he said.

"That something you learned in sociology class?" I asked.

"Psych 101. I've never actually taken a sociology class. Are you gonna survive without a babysitter?"

"Maybe. Maybe not. Look, before I lost my teaching job, I only drank a little on the weekends. You gotta blow off some steam. Granted, I've turned into Old Faithful lately, but I've gotta wash all this shit out of my head. Hopefully, someday I'll find some sort of peace. Or I won't. Who knows?"

"Go join one of those Jimmy Buffett retirement places or something—whatever it takes to keep that spark alive," he suggested.

"How old do you think I am?"

"Um..."

"Maybe in a couple of years," I said. "Although, that might be too much Parrot Head-ing even for me. In the meantime, I could be a manatee wrangler at Sea World or sweep the streets at Busch Gardens. They don't still have pirates in Florida, do they? Maybe they're hiring."

"I think there are some in Pittsburgh," he said.

"Too cold," I said.

"Well..."

"Before you go, as long as we're sharing. I talked to Sarah yesterday...for the last time, I imagine. I know you were wondering why—well—why they adopted JD and not you."

"Yeah?"

"One of you was sickly and in the hospital for a long time as a baby. It wasn't you. You weren't available. You already had a home. She didn't know about you. They didn't *choose* JD over you."

"I guess that's something," he said. "But why—"

"That's all I know, kid." I could have told him about Ronnie being his real father, but I no longer had to live up to being the most honest man in Possum Holler. I didn't have to be the most *anything* in Possum Holler, not even the biggest asshole. "But it ain't nothing. Drive safe."

"You, too. And don't drink and drive."

"Can I drink and *walk* when I get there?"

"From what I've seen, probably not, but what the hell? Give it a shot."

He waved and began backing up so that he could turn and drive forward along the driveway. I hopped in the truck and threw Jenny's letter into the glove compartment...just in case. I followed Jack's car to the end of the driveway and stopped to check the mailbox one last time. He gave me a weak thumb's-up, looked both ways, and rolled out onto Highway 228 for the final time. The little red car crept north, well below the speed limit. I figured he was collecting mental images for the cover of the novel that he swore he was not writing about the insane Southerners with whom he'd spent the summer and who'd managed to rip a new hole in his heart almost as soon as he'd patched the other. The joy of connecting with his brother had been squashed and yanked out by an emotional noose. In the same way that all the precious memories of my little girl were tainted because Riley no longer shared them with me, Jack's fraternal bond with JD also was a one-way street—permanently.

While my truck idled, I checked the mailbox. Nothing. I slammed it shut and stared at the old white country house with my hands dejectedly dug into my pockets. I no longer had a permanent address. Hell, I didn't even have a *temporary* address.

I thought of my maternal Granddaddy, not my paternal Amish one. After losing his legs to Nazi gunfire in World War II, he loved to play and sing train songs while indulging impossible fantasies of hopping a boxcar to the next town, whichever town that might be. It'd been more than four and a half decades since I'd last heard him strum a guitar and sing "King of the Road," but I finally understood the allure of hopping on an empty boxcar bound for anywhere. Unfortunately, trains roared through Possum Holler far too quickly for me to hop even with two good legs. Hell, it was all I could do to climb into my Tacoma lately without pulling a hammy. I felt a tear stream down my right cheek, though I had no coherent thoughts bouncing around in my head—just an overwhelming sense of failure and loss. I once loved that place. When we moved there a decade earlier, I thought I'd reached the finish line. Instead, it was my own personal sinkhole. All my happily-ever-after visions were swallowed up, and my life had gone to hell—or wherever the hell dreams go to die.

I surrendered in my staredown with the house and glared at Alyssa on the Flint Realty sign. I heard the rumble of thunder to my south, yonder way, the direction I was heading. I don't know why, but I took that thunder personally. If there was a big guy upstairs, he was mocking me. Granted, there was a lot to mock, but it didn't sit well. I kicked Alyssa in her perfectly straight white teeth, knocking the sign almost perpendicular to the ground. It felt good...for a second. I straightened up the sign so that someone could finally cash in on my mistake of trying to go home again. To me, this was where my concept of family began. For Riley, it was where families went to die. She would never make the mistake of returning to Possum Holler. It wasn't her home. Hell, it wasn't mine, either. Not anymore.

As I sat behind the wheel of the truck and cried while taking another long look at my shattered dreams, thunder rumbled once again. A steady rain followed Jack as he progressed northward, but the darkest clouds and brightest bolts of lightning to the south beckoned me like a champion boxer taunting his longshot challenger. I'd proven I could take a punch or two or fifty. When I was a kid, I sat in the living room alongside my dad as we watched heavyweight champ Larry Holmes deliver a brutal beating of Randall "Tex" Cobb in a title bout at the Astrodome. For 15 rounds, Holmes battered Cobb's face until it was grotesque. It amplified calls to reduce championship fights to 12 rounds. Yet, Cobb never hit the canvas. He'd smile and beg for more. He lost every single round on the scorecards. He later blamed his extensive brain damage on that one fight. That beatdown became his legacy. He flipped the script and turned the agony of defeat into the ecstasy of annihilation.

As the dark clouds preened, I smiled, just like Tex. If the storm wanted a piece of me, fine. It couldn't win. It could strike me with a firebolt or send my truck hydroplaning off the road and into a tree. Fine with me. Embrace the pain, I reminded myself. I floored the accelerator and raced south as massive rain drops pounded my windshield. I wanted to scream, but I wouldn't give the satisfaction to the unknown spirit above that had been screwing with me for its sick entertainment over the past several years. I was not going to throw in the towel like JD did. If the rest of my life was meant to be a slow-moving crash, then so be it. I looked skyward and addressed the brewing storm clouds with the calm resignation of an utterly defeated man who was stubbornly still standing, if only out of spite. What more could the omnipotent bastard have in store for me? Was there no war to solve somewhere? Some kid dying of cancer?

There was no peace for me on *this* side of the storm, not in Possum Holler. Who knew what awaited me on the other side? More misery? A sliver of hope, the one thing no one can live without? A fatal lightning bolt in the middle? There was only one way to find out.

"Bring it on," I calmly told the clouds ahead of me with a contemptuous smile. "Let's do this."

www.ingramcontent.com/pod-product-compliance
Lightning Source LLC
LaVergne TN
LVHW100519110826
845146LV00002B/694